GW00690735

Short Fiction fr

SOUTH INDIA

Short Fiction from
SOUTH INDIA
Kannada, Malayalam, Tamil, and Telugu

edited by
Subashree Krishnaswamy
and
K. Srilata
with an introduction by Mini Krishnan

OXFORD
UNIVERSITY PRESS

OXFORD
UNIVERSITY PRESS

YMCA Library Building, Jai Singh Road, New Delhi 110001

Oxford University Press is a department of the University of Oxford. It furthers
the University's objective of excellence in research, scholarship, and education
by publishing worldwide in

Oxford New York

Auckland Cape Town Dar es Salaam Hong Kong Karachi
Kuala Lumpur Madrid Melbourne Mexico City Nairobi
New Delhi Shanghai Taipei Toronto

With offices in

Argentina Austria Brazil Chile Czech Republic France Greece
Guatemala Hungary Italy Japan Poland Portugal Singapore
South Korea Switzerland Thailand Turkey Ukraine Vietnam
Oxford is a registered trade mark of Oxford University Press
in the UK and in certain other countries

Published in India
by Oxford University Press, New Delhi

ISBN-13: 978-0-19-569246-4
ISBN-10: 0-19-569246-2

Typeset in ElegantGarmond BT
by Mindways Design, Delhi 110 019
Printed at Ram Printgroph, Delhi 110 051
Published by Oxford University Press
YMCA Library Building, Jai Singh Road, New Delhi 110 001

Contents

Editors' Note

We have been involved with translations from the various Indian languages—teaching, editing, and conducting workshops—for quite a few years. We have noticed that though students and teachers at college level have responded with enthusiasm to our literatures, they have little access to resource material. Many teachers wished to include these literatures as part of the syllabus. There was a deeply felt need for a book that introduced students to our rich literary heritage.

In recent years, especially in the context of globalization, English has emerged as *the* most important link language in India. Indian literatures will therefore acquire a far wider readership even within the country if they are made available in English translation. Publishers and academics have begun to respond in different ways to this swiftly changing scenario.

This book has emerged after much discussion and deliberation. The texts have been chosen with care, keeping in mind some key issues. The interests of fresh undergraduates, who have not been exposed to such literatures, were a primary consideration. We tried out our selections on students to find that they were well received.

There is no *one* Indian experience. The urban is as much part of the Indian experience as the rural, humour is as much part of our lives as pathos, the life of the dalit is as authentic as that of the affluent, a woman's concerns as much part of humanity as a man's. We wanted our selection to encompass the whole range.

We designed the questions and activities at the end of each story with care. First of all, we wanted students to enjoy and appreciate the stories, to read and reread them several times to get the essence. We wanted them to notice what the authors were saying as well as how they were saying it. So our first set of questions—'Reading the Story'— reflects on the worldviews the texts offer and encourages students to look at nuances and connotations, to take note of vocabulary, style, imagery, theme, etc.

The second set of questions—'Translation Issues'—centres on pertinent issues in translation, especially the challenges that translated texts pose for both the translator and the reader. We would also like to draw attention to the fact that these are translated texts and not original writings, and that translation too is a creative process.

There is no point in teaching translation without encouraging students to try their hand at it. We also found that there is very little scope for creativity in our curriculum, so we decided to include a few activities that would tap creative potential. Our third set of questions—'Activities'—includes simple exercises in writing and translation.

We want the student to go beyond the text. Our questions are therefore not conventional. We hope that they equip students to interpret texts in different ways and experiment with a variety of critical approaches. The challenge, we feel, lies in reading outside of preconceived ideas and in questioning our most closely held beliefs. This can be unsettling but exciting.

We would like to thank OUP for giving us this opportunity to introduce literatures in translation to students. Thanks are also due to Mini Krishnan who conceived the idea and added special features to the book.

Subashree Krishnaswamy
K. Srilata

About the Editors

Subashree Krishnaswamy edited the *Indian Review of Books* for a number of years. She was also the editor of *Manas*, an imprint of East West Books, Chennai. *Manas* published translations from the various Indian literatures and many were critically acclaimed. Her book, *The Babel Guide to South Indian Fiction in Translation*, a book introducing Indian literatures to a western readership, is in the press. She is working on an anthology of young adult fiction in translation and is a Charles Wallace scholar. In 2005 she won the BBC Short Story Award for her work 'Bright Pink Butterfly Clips'.

K. Srilata teaches Literature in Translation and Creative Writing at IIT Madras. She has a Doctorate in women's writing and the Tamil print media from Central University, Hyderabad. She is the author of *The Other Half of the Coconut: Women Writing Self-Respect History* published by Kali for Women, New Delhi. She is also a poet. She won the first prize in the All India Poetry competition organized by the British Council and the Poetry Society, India, in 1997 and the Unisun-British Council poetry award in 2007. Her anthology of poems *Seablue Child* was published by Brown Critique, Kolkata. Srilata is a Charles Wallace scholar and a Fulbright pre-doctoral scholar.

Subashree and Srilata are also collaborating with Lakshmi Holmström on an anthology of Tamil poetry in translation.

Acknowledgements

The publisher wishes to thank the British Council for its support in developing this anthology and to acknowledge the following copyright holders for granting permission to reprint:

- Sahitya Akademi for 'A Sweet Dish'
- The British Council South Asian Women Writers Website for 'Seemantha'
- Samya Publications for 'Wooden Cradles'
- Orient Longman for 'The World Renowned Nose'
- East West Books for 'The Last Show', 'Squirrel', 'Rat', and 'The Chair'
- *The Week* and *Malayala Manorama* for 'The Touch'
- Professor Ranga Rao for 'Rain' and 'Taatayya (My Grandpa)'
- Professor Narayan Hegde for 'Annayya's Anthropology'

A special thanks to the British Council, *The Week*, and Narayan Hegde for granting permission gratis.

Introduction

This collection of stories is an attempt to introduce students to a great but unorganized body of work referred to as ILET – Indian Literature in English Translation. No reader of this book needs reminding that we live in a world of continuous communication in different languages—from manuals that accompany gadgets, to films from different countries, medicines, and bestsellers—made possible only by the act of translation. If anyone were to be hostile to the idea of translation s/he would be ignoring the deep human need to share thoughts and feelings. Translation is the natural extension of anything verbal and valuable that man wishes to communicate and it crosses three bridges—personal, linguistic, and cultural.

THE WORD AND THE WORLD

Language is like a city. To build this city, every human brings a stone. The beauty and durability of *vak*, logos, the word is what sets us apart from the rest of all creation. Language gives form to the store of human experience. It makes possible the stupendously vast memory bank of humankind—libraries of books going back hundreds of years; uncounted caches of documents and scripts; journals, diaries, letters, and reports, personal and official, that lie stored in both public and private collections. When words make up a book, a poem, a short story, a long story, a play, or a novel, they invite you to enter a city filled with secrets that then become your secrets and enrich your understanding of life.

WHAT IS TRANSLATION?

What exactly is translation? At a very simple level, when X who knows both English and Hindi meets Y who knows only English, and wants to tell Y '*Billi* mat *par chadhkar baithi*', X can very easily say, 'The cat sat on the mat', and not miss out on anything essential. If you were translating a legal document, the chief concern would be about conveying information correctly. One cannot, and one dare not, in translation, say that 'one side of the hill belongs to Mr XX' when the original document says that 'the *west* side of the hill, facing the river, belongs to Mr XX'. It is a matter of factual accuracy and the style and polish of language are irrelevant. But when a literary text is being translated from Oriya, Bengali, or Malayalam into English, all the complex layers of meaning concerning caste, rituals, and family ties become extremely difficult to convey in a language which originated in a country that has no cultural equivalents for the very *concepts* one sees in the Indian works. This is the difficulty that translators of Indian literary works face. There is no such thing called the caste system in an Anglocentric world, no such thing as a *yagna*, or being the head of a matrilineal household. So how do we go about translating, explaining, rewriting, recreating these local worlds in another word-world? How shall we reorder them, reread them from the perspective of global English and against a background of twenty-first century, Western book culture? That is when we arrive at a conclusion with which it is difficult to argue. Namely, that translating a literary text is like translating a culture, not just the words that appear in the language that has come out of that background. Sanskrit poetics offers us two terms to describe what translation is: *roopantar* and *anuvaad*. Roopantar means a change of form. Anuvaad means 'saying after' or 'explaining what comes after'. Taking things a bit further, Navalram, the Gujarati writer-reformist identified three types of translation: *shabdanusar* (word for word), *arthanusar* (sense to sense), and *rasanusar* (spirit to spirit).

OUR COUNTRY: AN ETHNIC MUSEUM

While India is a single entity politically, culturally it is subcontinental in nature. Our country is so complex and so diverse that it is impossible for a single person to assimilate and make generalizations. India has a vast and elaborate past and has lived with pluralisms for centuries. The history of India is based on linkages with not one civilization but three—Hindu, Islamic, and Christian—all traditional societies in which religion is the centre of daily community life.

Hinduism is so old and has so many dissenting viewpoints within itself that it is impossible to pin down its sources and growth. Islam reached India in two different ways: peacefully, through Arabs who came to the south-west coast as traders and violently, through Turkish and Afghan invaders who plundered the Indo-Gangetic plains and eventually stayed on to rule large parts of the subcontinent. India absorbed it all and has, over a thousand years, produced an influential and complex tradition of Islam. Some fifty years after the crucifixion of Jesus Christ, his message reached Kerala and when the first Europeans arrived on the south-west coast they were surprised to note the flourishing Syrian Christian tradition there. Besides this, for two centuries we have produced hybrid cultural practices out of our encounter with the modern West. This amazing capacity to assimilate alien elements is an essential feature of India. Standing outside the subcontinent's social class-structure is the adivasi (tribal) population. It keeps alive an oral literary culture, a great unwritten archive that calls for recording and translation. Equally marginalized and a painful sore on the face of the country is the 180 million dalit population that is only just finding a voice and a language in which to express itself.

THE LINGUISTIC LANDSCAPE OF INDIA

The complexity of India's language map is tremendous. There are fourteen major writing systems in use. No other country has five language families. We can count the Indo-Aryan, the Dravidian, the Austro-Asiatic, the Sino-Tibetan, and the Anadamanese. Some 400 languages are spoken, though the Census documents only 114. Of these, only eighteen enjoy official recognition and only some correspond to geographical boundaries. The hundreds of other mother tongues and dialects in the country lack the formal institutions that go with languages usually noticed, namely a publishing history, schools teaching in those languages, daily newspapers, and printing presses.

SOCIO-CULTURAL HISTORY OF INDIA

As you study the stories in this textbook, try to keep a few things in mind.

(i) For thousands of years before Christ, India was the continuous recipient of foreign influences. The earliest literary texts in the recorded history of India are in Tamil. Second comes Sanskrit, the language of migrating populations who came to India from somewhere in central Asia. While this *deva-bhasha* gradually became the language of Vedic philosophy and religious compositions, numerous local/regional traditions of folk-literature in languages that are not Sanskrit-based also existed simultaneously. Buddhist and Jain literatures were also composed in non-Sanskritic languages. This was roughly fifth–tenth centuries BC.

(ii) While the conquering Turks who established the Delhi Sultanate in the early thirteenth century ushered in a new era of political domination, they also enriched the region culturally when they introduced Arabic and Persian. India 'nativized' both and produced a hybrid language from it, namely Urdu. What is less well known is that thanks to the Arab traders on the Konkan coast and Malabar, and penetration into Chola land (the modern-day Tamil Nadu), there were brands of Tamilized Arabic and mixes of Malayalam and Tulu with Arabic, in South India, long before the thirteenth century.

(iii) Meanwhile, regional languages grew. Between the eleventh and fifteenth centuries, many languages like Bengali, Oriya, Assamese, Hindi, Kashmiri, Gujarati, Marathi, Telugu, Kannada, and Malayalam developed rich traditions in oral and written literature. Tamil continued to lead in sophistry and poetics of a very advanced order.

(iv) The British arrived in the seventeenth century to trade exactly like the Portuguese and French did before them. By the mid-nineteenth century, Britian's colonial embrace meant the supremacy of the English language. Universities and schools imposed a pattern of learning that had nothing to do with native traditions either Hindu or Islamic and that were alien to the spirit and genius of India. The demand for education in English came from social reformers like Raja Rammohan Roy who campaigned for it as part of his larger project of modernizing Indian society. G.N. Devy, one of our leading literary critics wrote, 'The English language was grafted onto India's linguistic banyan tree.'

(v) Missionary activity and translations of the Bible into Indian languages led to the preparation of dictionaries and the establishment of printing presses. With these tools came the spread of journals, magazines, and newspapers in local languages. This in turn generated a middle-class readership that wanted to read something other than stories and poems about gods and goddesses; they wanted to read about people like themselves. So forms and models found in English literature were quickly adapted by Indian writers during the nineteenth century. In this manner, a language that had no geographical base in India, became one of the mediums of our intellectual discourse and the means by which we began to communicate with the outside world.

Translation of Indian literature into English is only a little older than Indian writing in English. While literatures written in Indian languages enjoy a social base and cultural rootedness, the elitist nature of the use of English in India gives writing by Indians in English a 'national' character and the status of a national literature. Nevertheless, we should not view either of these categories with an air of prejudice. As Salman Rushdie said, 'Both drink from the same well, and India, that inexhaustible horn of plenty, nourishes us all.'

THE IMPORTANCE OF TRANSLATION

Translation jumps over oceans and travels in the time-machines of language. All intellectual transfers from ancient Phoenician, Chinese, Persian, and Greek civilizations to the present global-village and internet-oriented knowledge systems, have had to depend on people who moved—and can move—words, sentences, images, and themes from one language world to another. Although, in theory, you can translate *any* source text into *any* receiving language, the movement of literary texts is usually from an earlier language text to later languages, or from one contemporary language to another. For example nineteenth-century Bengali novels or twelfth century Telugu poetry are translated into twenty-first century English. It is unlikely that anyone will translate Harry Potter into Latin or *The God of Small Things* into Sanskrit though the latter has been translated into at least eighty modern world languages. If every book in Tamil or Gujarati or Oriya is a product of all the books in Tamil/Gujarati/Oriya that preceded it, what does it mean to be studying literary translation in a multi-ethnic, densely layered society like India? Why is it necessary to our sense of self that we should want not only to share our socio-lingual experiences with others by translating *our* literature but also seek to know what *their* experiences are like? The answer is that in a multi-lingual society like

India, translation is important because it is a form of promoting national understanding of the different regional 'selfs' in the country. Through literatures in translation, the development of a certain shared social vision is possible. Indeed one of the responsibilities of citizenship is to break out of a regional way of thinking and to feel involved in other linguistic cultures of the country. If freedom lies in knowing 'the other' and looking beyond the prison of the self, then translation is necessary for the emotional unshackling and well-being of our country. Why we, living in India, are proposing to study translations in English would be a logical question but we will come to that at the end of this introduction.

MOVEMENTS BETWEEN INDIAN LANGUAGES

Education in pre-colonial India was confined to certain castes and classes. Universal education was two centuries away and even vast numbers of rich and upper middle classes (certainly women) could not read or write much. Besides, ours was largely a strong and vibrant oral culture. Music and literature were in the form of songs and poems which moved from one language/region to another informally and easily. They were modified and enlarged as the fancy of the narrator dictated. Thus it is that there are so many versions of the *Bhagavata* stories and retellings of the Ramayana and the Mahabharata. Each is slightly different, with the major characters showing some regional peculiarities and preferences. Indeed, before Independence brought a sense of being a single nation, it was this fluid and travelling library of religious literary narrations that linked the loose confederation of India's linguistic regions. The *Kathasaritsagar* and the *Jataka* and *Hitopadesa* are also narratives that inspired the spread of hybrid stories. The clever wife, the foolish priest, and the greedy merchant are figures that appear in the lore of every region. This process of recomposition has always been our tradition.

INDIA AND THE WEST

Ancient literary texts of Mesopotamia, Greece, Persia, Alexandria/ Egypt, the Roman Empire, all reveal the world-mart of goods and philosophy that moved briskly between India and the Old World. But on 20 May 1498, when Vasco da Gama sailed into the port in Calicut he changed the course of history in our country because before him there was little or no direct contact between Europe and India. Hereafter it is important to take into account how significant India became as a possession to be understood, in order to be controlled and exploited.

The Contribution of Christian Missionaries

The earliest missionaries were British, German, Italian, and Portuguese Jesuits who were eager to spread the Gospel in Indian languages. They made enormous efforts to learn the local languages in order to translate the New Testament into them. They developed grammars and dictionaries and began the first translational exchanges between the classical languages (Tamil and Sanskrit) as well as the languages of the non-scholarly communities in India and European languages. Some time in the middle of the sixteenth century the first attempts were made in Goa to access Hindu texts. Father Thomas Stevens, a Jesuit who was sent to Goa in 1579, was astonished to learn that Konkani was a language spoken all along the Konkan coast but that it had no script. Even today it is written in Marathi, Kannada, Malayalam, Devnagari, and Roman—an unusual linguistic phenomenon. In 1615 he wrote a remarkable poem in Konkani called the *Christu Purana*. 'Like a jewel among pebbles, like a sapphire among jewels, is the excellence of the Marathi tongue.' It was a mix of Konkani and Portuguese and was written in the Marathi script.

A few decades earlier, Criminali and Henrique Henriques in the mid-sixteenth century had expressed themselves ably in Tamil. In 1554 a Tamil–Portuguese Christian manual appeared in Lisbon, the 'first ever book to be printed in any Indian language'. But Roberto de Nobili (1577–1656), Bartholomaus Zieganbalg (1682–1719), and Heinrich Roth (1620–68) were pioneers who actually lived amongst Indians, learnt their languages first hand, developed linguistic tools, and made a study of their culture. Roth developed the first Sanskrit grammar in Latin in the seventeenth century. For our purposes it is also interesting to note that the first example of a Sanskrit text being translated into a European language is that of Bhartrhari's poems appearing in German in 1663 and in French in 1670.

European Traders and Language

The year 1583 brought the first British traders who gradually overcame, in turn, first the Portuguese and then the French to become the sole white traders in India. They came not as scholars or travellers but as merchants and as such were not at all interested in the culture or religion of the country. If the Europeans studied any language here, it was Persian because it was the court language and because they had to conduct trade with Mughal outposts. The role of people who knew two languages became critical. Such a person was known as a '*dwibhashi*', that is a speaker of two languages.

THE MUGHALS AND TRANSLATION

Under the Mughals, when Persian became the court language (the ruler's language though not the ruling language), Sanskrit and Hindu literature along with Buddhist and Jain began to retreat. However, just as many centuries before, Alexander the Great had persuaded the scholars of conquered countries to translate their scrolls for his huge library in Alexandria, the Mughal emperor Akbar set up a translation bureau in India in the sixteenth century. He was genuinely interested in making Indian thought available in Persian. His goal was to promote harmony between the two major religious systems of the day and he wanted his nobles to understand the Hindu population that they ruled. The first translation of the Ramayana came from a Maulvi named Badayuni (1580). Akbar also arranged for the Mahabharata, the *Yogavasistha*, the *Harivamsa*, and the *Bhagavata* to be translated. So it was through Persian that the West first became acquaninted with the language and sacred literature of the Hindus.

THE IMPORTANCE OF DARA SHIKOH

It is important to note a few more milestones in order to get a basic idea of language politics and how it affected the formal development of literary translation in India. We skip two generations of Mughal rulers and come to Shah Jahan's eldest son Prince Dara Shikoh who was keenly interested in Hinduism and who commissioned the translation of fifty Upanishads into Persian. Dara's goal was to arrive at a social and religious common ground of what he called *asmani kitab* (heavenly books). When Dara was executed by Aurangzeb in 1659, the plan fell apart. Some years later the French traveller Bernier, who was collecting silk carpets, brassware, and jewellery came along and carried off this Persian translation to Europe as a curio, a collector's item. There it lay forgotten for more than a hundred years till the French scholar

Anquetil-Duperron came upon it and translated it into a strange mix of Latin, Greek, and Persian in 1801.

THE ENGLISH LANGUAGE IN INDIA

Colonial education brought with it the establishment of English literature in India. A look at the pattern of marks awarded for the Indian Civil Service examinations in the middle of the nineteenth century is revealing. For English and English history—1500; for Greek and Latin—1500; for mathematics—1250; for the natural sciences—500; for logic and philosophy—500; for French, German, Italian, Sanskrit, Persian, and Arabic—only 375 each. Thus great importance was accorded to English studies. Since the path of advancement was clear, tutoring in schools was also influenced by what would be required later. This led to another irreversible reality: from the times of Raja Rammohan Roy, well into the twentieth century, Anglicization was viewed as an achievement, and a knowledge of English was equated with progress and modernization.

CULTURAL DOMINATION OF ENGLISH IN INDIA

When the Maratha wars ended in the early nineteenth century, the English rulers, first in the form of the East India Company and later the Crown, saw themselves in the role of a superior race, nation, and civilization. The most important face of this new superiority was the English language, which, through the British Raj, established its hold over India's cultural world. Exactly like Sanskrit, Arabic, and Persian in India, it was Latin and Greek that were the classical languages of British universities and the language of the scholarly classes. English literature was not taught as a university subject in Britain till the late nineteenth century, but was promoted as the symbol of civilization for the Indian colony; its study was institutionalized in India (by 1860 one could get a BA Hons in English from Calcutta University) before it was in England (Oxford University, 1894). When the British introduced English in Indian schools and colleges, they had an imperial plan: 'The grandeur, the moral, and humanistic values of English literature would extort a willing consent to British rule' (J. Farish of the Bombay Presidency, 1838). They believed that when someone studied English literature he or she would not be able to help admiring that body of work and would, as a natural extension of this, become admirers of British culture. They were right. For 200 years, Indian languages, literature, and art forms took a beating from which they are yet to recover. Many generations of Indians genuinely believed that Indian literature and culture had nothing to match the scale, delicacy, or greatness of things British. When our intelligentsia began to look down upon all things Indian, when India retreated subserviently before the confident advance of Western influences which included modern science, we truly became a subject race.

We were even ready to believe as so many still do, that it was through European missionaries that Christianity reached India. Social thinkers have likened this state of our history to a massive amnesia, a cultural forgetfulness.

COLONIAL LANGUAGE ADVENTURES

For the first hundred years, translations of Indian texts into English were prepared by Englishmen in collaboration with Indians. Why did they undertake such translations? British scholars urged their government to discover, collect, and translate information about the land the East India Company was controlling. In documents dated 1783 and 1788, they referred to the hidden value of 'the ancient works of the Hindoos'. The Governer-General Warren Hastings (in office from 1772 to 1785) felt that Hindus should be governed by Hindu laws. He had the law books (*dharmashastras*) translated from Sanskrit into Persian by Indians. Then Englishmen translated the Persian versions into English. The final texts were very difficult to appreciate, the reader having to wrestle with a knotty mixture of the language of the original text, the in-between mosaic, and the final target-language renderings.

The first translation brought into being in this fashion using a 'broker-language' (Persian) between Sanskrit and English, was a legal text *Vivadarnavasetu* (meaning across the sea of litigation), which appeared under the name, *A Code of the Gentoo Laws* (1776) translated by Nathaniel Halhed.

We must now look at one of the most brilliant men of the eighteenth century: William Jones (1746–94). By the time he arrived in India as a judge of the Supreme Court in Calcutta in 1783, he was already a famous Persian scholar. On 1 January 1784, he founded the Asiatic Society with himself as president and Warren Hastings (Governor-General of India) as its patron. William Jones had three ambitions. He wished to publicize Indian culture and play the role of India's literary ambassador; he wanted to educate and improve the condition of 'the natives'; he wanted European interpretations (translations) of Hindu laws because he felt that his Indian assistants could not be relied on to interpret the law accurately or fairly. As it was, the British were dependant on Indian scholars and lawyers as they themselves did not know Sanskrit. Before the nineteenth century began, William Jones produced his famous translation of the *Manusmriti* (the Code of Manu), the law-book of the Hindus. Beginning with a publication that was printed and circulated privately, William Jones' *The Ordinances of Manu* quickly went through four editions and reprints that lasted nearly a hundred years right uptil 1880. Meanwhile his English translation of many short poems from Sanskrit and finally Kalidasa's famous play *Abhijnanashakuntalam* appeared in 1789. Known as *Shakuntala* (or *The Fatal Ring*), it dazzled both British and German readers when it was translated into German two years later.

THE IMPORTANCE OF GERMAN SCHOLARSHIP

Around the time that William Jones' writings about India were being admired, the translated Upanishads that Dara Shikoh had commissioned (in the 1560s) and which Duperron had worked on in the year 1800–1 (see page xxi here) caught the attention of the German philosopher Schopenhauer. At exactly this time also, a young poet-philosopher named Friedrich von Schlegel, who was studying Sanskrit under an Englishman in Paris, was so moved by what he learnt, that on his return to Germany he published *On the Language and Wisdom of the Indians* (1808). This sudden discovery of a vast body of literature in a sophisticated and advanced language that had remained unknown for so many centuries sent a tremor through the libraries of Europe. A.L. Basham says that it was like the discovery of classical literature that had influenced learning some centuries before; but it was a greater shock than the Renaissance because the 'new' texts came from a land which had, uptil that time, been considered primitive and pagan, even outlandish. It is worth remembering that in keeping with our finest syncretic traditions, the first person who tried to build a bridge between two entirely different—even hostile— traditions was a Mughal prince. It should also be noted that the next leap between literary worlds was made possible only because of translation; and, indeed, the first public unlocking of the grandeur of Indian philosophy came from Germany, a country that had no imperial designs on India, or in denigrating Indian genius or intellectuality. It is worth remembering Schopenhauer's words, 'That incomparable book stirs the spirit to the very depths of the soul. In the whole world there is no study so beneficial and so elevating as that of the Upanishads [he called it Oupnekhat]. It has been the solace of my life, it will be the solace of my death.'

William Jones was the first British scholar to see that India had a literary culture worth studying; thereafter the spreading outward of Indian literatures to the rest of the subcontinent and beyond was unstoppable. The brisk practice of translation that Jones, Wilkins, and the Orientalists began at that time, opened up a new area of scholarship which came to be called Indology. It even became fashionable for the English in India to learn about India! But after the 1857 Indian Uprising failed, Indology went into decline because the British government took over from the East India Company and began to suppress all things Indian. The Raj, which lasted ninety years politically, and at least another couple of decades culturally, had begun.

EARLY TRANSLATIONS

In 1785, Charles Wilkins prepared the first direct translation into English of a Sanskrit text. Can you guess what that text was? It was the Bhagavad Gita. (He called it the *Bhagavet Geeta*.) In the last forty years of the nineteenth century, Indians began translating their own classics. A hundred years after *Shakuntala* appeared in German (translated in 1791 from the English rendering), Mohini Chatterji's translation of the Gita was co-published by Ticknor and Co., Houghton and Miffin, and the Riverside Press. English had launched India in the Western world. It was only in the generation of Tagore and Aurobindo Ghosh that the practice of translating *contemporary* Indian works into English began. After Tagore's *Gitanjali* won the Nobel Prize for Literature (1913), Indian writers began to feel that they *had* to be seen in English translation. Then bloomed the challenges of translation within the Indian tradition. This introduced the preoccupations of Western ideas of translation to us. Although a great deal of Western art and civilization is based on translations of the Christian gospels and related religious texts, translation in Europe was considered an inferior activity, some sort of secondary form of scholarship. This opinion though still prevalent in India, is fading. Both writers and scholars of literature are beginning to view translations with respect. They see that every text is a fabric to be considered from all angles, to be shredded and woven together in fresh word combinations that would strongly echo the old pattern but appear in terms of renewed creativity. Translation is being viewed as a rebirth of texts and ideas and not a mere xerox, a pale copy, a feeble echo. It is seen as being the recreation of an already existing text as a new work in a language in which it could never have been envisaged.

IWE AND ILET

There is a difference between Indian writers in English (IWE) and Indian regional-language writers who appear in English (ILET). The former have already translated themselves. They are writing for readers whose mental picture-galleries hold only those words that describe, match, and link up Indian experiences in English without hitting speedbreakers. Many discomforts can be explained away in the body of the text itself, such as. 'She took care not to touch the pooja items *because she was in her period, a condition considered polluting.*' In a regional-language text, the second half of the sentence wouldn't be present at all *because there would be no need to explain why the pooja items had to be left untouched.* In an English translation of a regional-language work, these lines would mystify the non-Indian reader who would be unaware of this custom in Hindu households, but not a single Indian, no matter what his or her religion, would need the explanation. This is the reason Indian writing in English is so attractive to those readers outside India who cannot read our languages but yearn for the exotic and layered flavours of the material aspects of our country. They are under a powerful illusion that these Indian flavours are reaching them in English.

ENGLISH AND INDIAN LANGUAGES

The list of languages in India with more than 1,00,000 native speakers of each, numbers about ninety. Of these, English is not even among the first fifty! Yet we are looking at the possibility of studying some of our writers who have been translocated in English. Why? History favours this language almost unfairly. The Central Sahitya Akademi of India, which promotes and awards writing in twenty-four languages has a library of reference books unmatched for the breadth and scope of their research. Its literary periodical, *Indian Literature*, is in its fiftieth year of publication. What language do all these works appear in?—English. Why do you think this is so?— Arranged as we are into states that were demarcated on the basis of the predominant languages in those regions, the fact is that we live on literary and language islands. Just because most of us feel safe in this island culture does not make it any healthier. The windows of Andhra Pradesh let in non-Indian literature but not Tamil or Malayalam literature. A look at the bookshops in any railway station will serve to convince one on this point. The fact is that, of all the languages we use, English is the medium of the widest literary exchange among Indians, and it offers an all-India participation on a scale that no other language can, at present. That so many decades after Independence this continues unaltered, is a matter of some concern to some social philosophers and language chauvinists.

INDIANS, INDIAN LITERATURE, AND ENGLISH

English in India defines India's contact with the English-speaking world in both positive and negative ways. Positively, by creating a class of English-speaking Indians who control the resources of literacy and knowledge in English, including science. Negatively, by promoting a new element of separation between this elite group and non-English-speaking Indians. For a body of writing to become great, it needs to develop from a language that is rooted in the soil, and that grows organically from people's experiences. The culture embodied in original writing in English is of recent origin in India and has a short history of a little over a hundred years whereas strong regional linguistic cultures emerged in different parts of India at least ten centuries ago. But in order to *integrate* our experiences from different regions in different languages, we need to plunge over and over again into a pool where the norms are recongnizable. And this pool is the English language. So we use the linguistic experience of the English language to bring out the cultural experience of our regional languages. In the words of the literary genius, Raja Rao, 'The telling has not been easy. One has to convey in a language that is not one's own the spirit that is one's own.' This mantra has to be enlarged for translation. The literature in regional languages can hardly become 'national' until it is disseminated in English translation; so, as Aijaz Ahmad said, English is bound to become 'the language in which the knowledge of "Indian" literature is produced.' As students of literature it would expand our horizons if we study English literature as well as our own literatures in English translation to develop perspectives and interpretations to learn about ourselves and about the emotional and social forces that shape us.

INDIANS TRANSLATING INTO ENGLISH

A document released by the British Council in India's fiftieth year of Independence predicted that the future of English lies in the minds of its non-native users. That statement is worth remembering in the light of the fact that the best translations in world literature usually appear in the translator's own language/mother tongue. Will English soon be the mother tongue of many Indians? The answer to that question is two questions. One, hasn't it already become so? And, two, is there not a sizable population in our country that does all its reading and writing in English and no other language? It is important to understand how Indo-English translators have reversed the basic condition of successful translations, and blasted their way through norms, thereby becoming some of the most unique people in the literary firmament. While they read in a certain language, the consciousness absorbs and operates bilingually, a strange, powerful capacity of the human brain.

THE FUTURE: MORE AND MULTIPLE TRANSLATIONS

Since language is continually changing and developing, it is possible to see the same work translated by more than one person. This is the nature of translations. They are never final. Many works are (re)translated over and over again to make their language contemporary. Religious literature is a prime example as also famous works that are perennial favourites. The reason they continue to be perennial favourites is that they are freshly translated every ten years or so. In the great debate between hegemonic global cultures— predominantly Western—and nationalism, we must ascertain that local knowledge, local genius, and local achievement are given their due importance. If we do not read and position our writers, it would be a cultural failure on our part like allowing our heritage buildings to be destroyed or permitting our crafts to vanish.

TRANSLATION: A DANGEROUS ACTIVITY

Translation of any kind leads to a better understanding in a person or group who did not or could not previously follow something prepared in someone else's language (let's call it a 'foreign' language). Since knowledge and information systems have always been sources of power, any translation/transfer has always been seen as a threat to *someone*. The priests, the kings, the medicine men, all guarded their scrolls and texts as well as they guarded their positions in life. Today the Bible in any world language is freely available; but there was a time when it was not available even in English from which it has been translated into all the Asian and African languages. Its translation from Aramaic and Greek into German and English was violently opposed by both the Church and the rulers; translators like Wycliffe and Tyndale were hunted down, imprisoned, and burnt to death.

CONCLUSION

India is a post-colony still reconciling her traditional past with modernity and arriving at different hybrids in different parts of the country.

African novelist Ngugi Wa Thiongo in an analysis of the politics of language identifies the 'cultural bomb' as a weapon of colonialism that destroys a people's belief in their names, their languages, in their capacity, and ultimately in themselves. Our reconstruction of our history must therefore include a sense of cultural nationalism that lies hidden in our enormously rich literature; translating it into English should be one of the social and literary goals of this century, and studying it one of the keys to reaching a vision of our Indian identity.

It was translation into English that gave us our first literary superstar—Tagore—and he said, 'Civilization is built on man's surplus.' Let us nurture this surplus of which we have such abundance.

Mini Krishnan

References

Ahmad, Aijaz, 1993. *In Theory: Classes, Nations, Literatures*, New Delhi: Oxford University Press.

Amirthanayagam, Guy, 2000. *The Marriage of Continents,* University Press of America.

Basham, A.L., 1957. *Culture and Civilization of India*, New Delhi: Oxford University Press.

Bassnett, S., 1980 [1991]. *Translation Studies*, London and New York: Routledge.

Das, S.K., 1991. *A History of Indian Literature: Western Impact: Indian Response 1800–1910*, Vol. III, New Delhi: Sahitya Akademi.

Devi, G.N., 1993. *In Another Tongue: Essays on Indian English Literature*, Chennai: Macmillan India Limited.

—— 1998. *Of many Heroes: An Indian Essay in Literary Historiography*, Mumbai: Orient Longman.

Dingwaney, A. and C. Maier (eds), 1996. *Between Languages and Cultures*, New Delhi: Oxford University Press.

Joshi, S. (ed.), 1991 [1992]. *Rethinking English: Essays in Literature, Language, History,* New Delhi: Oxford University Press.

Kothari, Rita, 2003. *Translating India,* UK: St Jerome Publishing.

Metcalf, T., 1995. *Ideologies of the Raj: The New Cambridge History of India*, London: Cambridge University Press.

Mukherjee, S., 1994. *Translation as Discovery*, Hyderabad: Orient Longman.

Nair, R.B. (ed.), 2002. *Translation Text and Theory: The Paradigm of India*, New Delhi and London: Sage Publications.

Narasimhaiah, C.D., 1969. *The Swan and the Eagle*, Simla: Indian Institute of Advanced Study.

Ngugi Wa Thiongo, 1986. *Decolonising the Mind: The Politics of Language in African Literature*, London: Heinemann.

Niranjana, T., 1992. *Siting Translation: History, Post-Structuralism and the Colonial Context*, Hyderabad: Orient Longman.

Raja Rao, 1988. 'Entering the Literary World', *World Literature Today*.

Rushdie, S., 1991. *Imaginary Homelands*, London: Granta Books in association with Penguin India.

The British Council, UK, 1992. *The Future of English*.

Viswanathan, G., 1989. *Masks of Conquests: Literary Study and British Rule in India*, London: Faber and Faber.

KANNADA

KUM. VEERABHADRAPPA (b. 1951)

Kum. Veerabhadrappa or Kum. Vee is well known for his controlled handling of sensitive themes. His writings, brilliantly crafted, force the reader to think about important issues such as oppression and inequality. His stories, as in the collection *Bari Katheylloo Anna,* are often about the feudal culture so prevalent in our country. They are stories of protest. Yet, they touch upon the intricacies of human relations. They are all the more effective because they are neither preachy nor didactic. His consummate skill as a writer shines through in every story.

ಹುಗ್ಗಿ

ಅಪ್ಪ ಬಂದ ಎಂದು ಕೇಳಿ ಬಸವ ಒಂದೇ ಉಸಿರಿಗೆ ಚಣ್ಣ ಏರಿಸಿಕೊಂಡು ಹೊಸ್ತಿಲುದಾಟಿದ್ದ. ನಿನ್ನೆಯಿಂದ ಹೊಟ್ಟೆ ಚುರುಗುಟ್ಟುತ್ತಿದ್ದುದರಿಂದ ಈ ದಿನ ಅಪ್ಪನೇನಾದರೂ ತಂದಿರಬಹುದೆಂದು ಅವನ ಲೆಕ್ಕ. ಅಪ್ಪ ಕಟ್ಟೆಯ ಒಂದು ವಕ್ಕ ಕುಸ್ಮರುಗಾಲಿಲೆ ಕುಂತುಕೊಂಡು ಬೆಳಿಗ್ಗಿ ಅರ್ಧ ಸೇದಿ ಬಿಟ್ಟಿದ್ದ ಬೇಡಿಯನ್ನು ಓಂಗಿರುವ ತುಟಿ ನಡುವೆ ಸಿಟ್ಟಿಸಿಕೊಂಡು ಕಡ್ಡಿಗೀರಿದ. ಅಪ್ಪನ ಮುಖ ಯಾಕ ಸಪ್ಪಗ್ತಿ ಎಂಬುದರ ಬಗ್ಗೆ ಬಸವ ಯೋಚಿಸಿದನಾದರೂ ಅರ್ಥವಾಗಲಿಲ್ಲ. ನಾನ್ ಕಂಡ್ಹೂಡ್ಲೆ ಬೆನ್ನು ಸಪ್ಪಿ ಐದು ಪೈಸೆ ಹತ್ತು ಕೊಡ್ತಿದ್ದ ಅಪ್ಪ ಈ ಹೊತ್ತು ಯಾಕೆ ಹಂಗಿದ್ದಾನಿ? ಎಂದು ಬಸವನ ವಾಲಿಗೆ ದೊಡ್ಡ ಸಮಸ್ಯೆಯಾಗೆ ಉಳಿಯಿತು. ಒಂದೊಂದೇ ಹೆಜ್ಜೆ ಇಡುತ್ತ ಅಡುಗೆ ಮನೆಬಾಗಿಲು ದಾಟದ ಕೂಡಲೆ ಅಲ್ಲಿ ನಡೆಯುತ್ತಿರುವುದನ್ನು ನೋಡಿ ಉಬ್ಬಿ ಹೋದ. ಎರಡು ಮೊರೆಗಳಲ್ಲಿ ಬೆಲ್ಲ, ಕಲ್ಲಿ ಬೇಳೆ ಇದ್ದವು. ಕಲ್ಲಿ ಬೇಳೆ ಮೊರ ಹಿಡಿದುಕೊಂಡು ಹಸನು ಮಾಡಿಕೊಡಗಿದ ಅಮ್ಮನ ಬೆನ್ನ ಮೇಲೆ ಬಿದ್ದು ಅಮ್ಮ ಈ ಹೊತ್ತು ಉಣ್ಣಾಕ ಏನ್ಮಾಡ್ತಿ? ಎನ್ನುತ್ತ ಸಪ್ಪಳವಿಲ್ಲದಂತೆ ಒಂದು ಬೆಲ್ಲದ ಚೂರನ್ನು ಎತ್ತಿಕೊಂಡು ಬಾಯಲ್ಲಿ ಹಾಕಿಕೊಂಡ. ನಿನ್ನೆಯಿಂದ ನೀರು ಕೂಡಾ ಕಂಡಿರದಿದ್ದ ಹೊಟ್ಟೆ ಆ ಬೆಲ್ಲದ ಚೂರಿನಿಂದ ತಂಪಿ ಹೋದಂತೆನಿಸ್ತು. ಆ ಬೆಲ್ಲದ ಮೊರ ಸುತ್ತ ಚಂದ್ರ, ಕೊಟ್ರ, ತಿಮ್ಮಿ ಮೂವರೂ ಅಮ್ಮಗೆ ಹೆದರಿ ಬರೀ ಜೊಲ್ಲು ಸುರಿಸುತ್ತ ಕುಂತಿದ್ದರು. ಅಮ್ಮನ ಮೊಲಿಗಳು ಎದೆಗಂಟ ಬತ್ತಿಹೋಗಿದ್ದರಿಂದ ತಿಮ್ಮಿ ಮೊಲಿ ಎಂದು ಆತ್ತರೆ ಸಾಕು ಅಮ್ಮ ಚಟ್ಟಂತ ಕಿನ್ನಿಗೆ ಬಾರಿಸಿ ಮೂರೆಕ್ಕೆ ತಳ್ಳಿ ಗುಸುಗುಟ್ಟುತ್ತಿದ್ದಳು. ಈಗ ಅಮ್ಮನೇ ತಿಮ್ಮಿಯನ್ನು ಎದೆಗವುಚಿಕೊಂಡು ಆಳತೊಡಗಿದ್ದು ಕಂಡು ಬಸವನಿಗೆ ಆಶ್ಚರ್ಯವಾಯಿತು. ಹಿಂಗ್ಯಾಕ ಆಳತಾಳ ಅಮ್ಮ ಎಂದು ಮಗ್ನು ತುಂಬಿದ ತಲೆಯನ್ನು ಕೆರೆಮಕೊಂಡನಾದರೂ ಉತ್ತರ ಸಿಗಲಿಲ್ಲ. ಇನ್ನೊಂದು ಚೂರು ಬೆಲ್ಲಕ್ಕೆ ಕೈ ಹಚ್ಚಿ ಅಮ್ಮಾ ಈ ಹೊತ್ತು ಉಣ್ಣಾಕ ಎಸ್ ಮಾಡ್ತಿ? ಎಂದು ಸ್ವಲ್ಪ ಗಟ್ಟಿಯಾಗಿಯೇ ಕೇಳಿದ. ಕಣ್ಣುಗಳ ತಗ್ಗಿನಿಂದ ಜಿನುಗುತ್ತಿದ್ದ ನೀರನ್ನು ಹರಿದಿದ್ದ ಸೆರಿಗಿನ ಚೊಂಗಿನಿಂದ ನೀರನ್ನು ಒರಿಸಿಕೊಳ್ಳುತ್ತ ಹುಗ್ಗಿ ಎಂದಳ್ಳೇ ಅಂದು ಮೂರೆಕ್ಕೆ ತಲೆ ತಗ್ಗಿಸಿದಳು. ಇದನ್ನು ಕೇಳಿ ಬಸವ ಮನಸ್ಸಲ್ಲಿಯೇ ಹುಗ್ಗಿ ಹುಗ್ಗೀ ಎಂದು ಮೂರು ನಾಲ್ಕು ಬಾರಿ ಅಂದು ಕೊಂಡು ಖುಷಿಪಟ್ಟ, ಹುಗ್ಗಿ ಹೊಡೆಯುವುದನ್ನು ಬೀಮ, ಕೊಟ್ಟ ಎಲ್ಲರಿಗೂ ಹೇಳಿ ಬರಬೇಕೆಂದುಕೊಂಡ. ಚಣ್ಣ

A Sweet Dish*

When Basava heard that his father was back, he quickly adjusted his loose shorts and ran in. His belly had been burning with hunger for a whole day and he hoped his father had brought home something to eat. He saw him sitting on his haunches at the edge of the *katta* with a half-smoked bidi in his mouth, striking a match. 'Why is father's face so dull?' wondered Basava but could not find an answer. 'Why doesn't he pat me and give me a five or ten paise coin, as he usually does when he sees me?' This was an unresolved question for Basava. He slowly walked towards the kitchen. What he saw there filled him with joy. His mother was cleaning split Bengal gram in a *mora* and there was another mora by her side full of jaggery pieces. 'What will you cook today, *Amma*?' he asked her as he picked up a piece of jaggery and put it in his mouth. The jaggery seemed to fill his empty stomach. Chandra, Kotra, and Thimmi sat round the mora with their mouths watering but afraid to touch the jaggery for fear of punishment. Amma's breasts had gone dry and flat and whenever Thimmi tried to feed, she would strike her and push her away. But now she held her close to her bosom and wept. 'Why is Amma crying like this?' Basava asked himself but could not think of an answer. He picked up another piece of jaggery and asked her again, 'Amma, what will you cook for us today?' '*Huggi*', Amma replied, wiping her tears away with the end of her torn sari and hiding her face with the mora. The mental repetition of the word huggi made Basava very happy. 'I must break this news to Bhima, Sochha, and others,' he said to himself and came out into the verandah, where his father was seated. Father called him and made him sit by his side. '*Appa* is crying because he is unable to provide us with food,' Basava said to himself glancing at his face. His father took out a ten paise coin from his pocket and gave it to Basava. The sight of the shining coin which filled his palm cheered Basava. He jumped up and ran towards

*Huggi

Sochha's house. Sochha was standing under the neem tree, winding a string round his top. 'You starving bastard,' Sochha had called him the day before. Basava showed him the coin in his hand and boasted: 'Sochha, do you know something? We are cooking huggi in our house today.' Sochha released his top from the string and was indifferent. 'Jealous son of a bitch,' Basava said to himself and walked towards Enkappa Shetty's shop. Shetty was resting against the cash box and sliding the sacred thread up and down his back. Basava pushed the coin towards him and asked for roasted gram. 'Rama, Rama,' said Shetty, as he filled a small measure with the gram and emptied it into Basava's shirt pocket. Basava put a few grains in his mouth, but restrained himself. He was afraid he would lose his appetite for huggi. Holding his pocket tightly so that the gram didn't spill out, he ran back to his house.

When Basava entered the house panting for breath, it was black with smoke. He thought it must be the smoke which had brought tears to his father's eyes. Chandra, Kotra, and Thimmi were all crying for jaggery. Water flowed from their mouths and noses. The oven was spitting waves of smoke and his mother coughed as she blew through the pipe into it. Her bones showed through the torn blouse at the back and Basava suppressed his desire to embrace her from the back. Fire slowly stretched its slender tongue through the smoke and she lifted her face and wiped her nose with her sari. She looked at Basava and let out a big sigh. Basava gave some of the gram to his brothers and sister and went and sat by his father's side. Thoughts of huggi danced through his mind and he looked in utter incomprehension at the blank faces of his father and mother, who seemed to have lost their speech all of a sudden. His brothers and sister were still crying. They were hungry and clamouring for huggi. 'When will it be ready, Amma?' Basava asked. 'Soon. Have some patience,' his father said, placing a comforting hand on his back.

His mother powdered the jaggery and put it in a vessel placed on the noisy oven. Basava had exhausted all his roasted gram and his mind was fixed on huggi. He had a hard time swallowing the saliva which filled his mouth at the thought of the sweet dish. His father began to talk to him. 'Basava, we are all going away from this village. You'll live in the Gowda's house. I have arranged it with him,' he said. Basava was thunderstruck at his father's words. 'No, I won't live in Gowda's house.

I'll also come with you,' he wailed, shaking his father by his shoulders. He noticed that his parents were exchanging meaningful looks and became alert. He remembered his father telling Nijlinga the other day that he was planning to go to Hospet to make a living. 'There is nothing but hunger and death in this place. We should go away,' his father had said to his mother just the day before, when she was busy boiling the rice for *conjee*.

Basava was frightened but the thought of huggi that was cooking in the oven made him forget everything else. When his mother picked up a stick to stir the mixture in the vessel, Chandra, Kotra, and Thimmi started fighting for plates. Basava too entered the fray and managed to secure a battered aluminium plate. They all sat staring at the vessel in the oven. Father's face resting on his raised knees was blank. Basava heard his deep sighs but huggi commanded all his attention. His mother picked up a piece of blackened cloth in her hands and lifted the vessel off the oven. The sweet smell invaded their nostrils causing tremendous excitement. All of them pushed their plates forward and demanded to be served first, but mother was looking elsewhere. 'Amma, give me huggi,' Basava pushed his plate right in the face of his mother and when she said, 'Go first to Gowda's place and return the metal vessel; don't be childish,' he could not control his anger and tears. 'I am hungry. I'll go after my meal,' he insisted. 'Let him have a little huggi,' said his father intervening and Basava was very happy. His mother put two spoonfuls of huggi on his plate and said, 'Enough. Now be off.' But Basava pressed for more and got it. The huggi was still very hot; he had to cool it with his breath and he could eat it only in small morsels.

'What if I had to starve for two days. I got this sweet dish at last,' Basava told himself as he cleaned the plate deftly with his fingers.

When he started harassing his mother for another helping she said firmly, 'Enough for now. Go and deliver this vessel at the Gowda's place'. Basava refused to go but when his father threatened to kick him if he didn't, he picked up the heavy vessel and stepped out of the house. He was worried whether any huggi would be left by the time he returned. 'I must be quick,' he said to himself and was about to break into a run when he heard his mother calling out to him.

She was standing at the door with her mouth covered by the end of her sari. Basava thought for a moment that she would let him have more of the huggi, but she just cried silently. She called him to her side and put her hand on his head and said just one word, 'Go.' Basava looked at his mother's tear-stained face and asked, 'Amma, why are you crying?' When there was no answer, he picked up the vessel and walked briskly towards the Gowda's house. He didn't forget to say, 'Amma, save some huggi for me.' If his mother had insisted that he should go before eating he would not have known what to do. For two days he had had no food; leave alone the vessel he couldn't have carried even his own body.

When Basava approached the corner round Tayavva's temple, he saw Bhima and wanted to talk to him. 'Where are you off to, Bhima?' he asked him and deliberately let out a loud belch. But Bhima didn't oblige him by asking what he had eaten and so he volunteered the information. 'We had a feast of huggi today,' and hastened towards Gowda's house. He knew the shortest route to the place as he used to accompany his mother every day when she went there to clean the vessels. He enjoyed eating the leftovers which his mother passed on to him. There were moments when he was moved to tears at the sight of his mother reduced to the size of a sparrow in the midst of large piles of vessels.

Basava stopped apruptly when he saw the brown dog guarding the barbed wire gate of the Gowda's house. But the dog recognized him and wagged his tail, which gave him courage. His body was tense with fear as he entered the gate. He crossed the cattleshed and climbed the steps leading to the verandah. As he lowered his burden on the floor, Gowda who was lying in an easy chair, called out to him, 'Basya, when are you coming here to live? Your father has talked to me.' He looked fiercer than the dog. Basava was frightened. He moved a couple of steps backward and said, 'Mother has asked me to return quickly,' and was about to leave when Gowda rose from his chair and stopped him, 'Where can you go now? Your father has bound you to me in settlement of his debts. You'll not find your parents at home. They should have gone away by now.' Basava shook with fear. He wanted to cry loudly, but when he looked at Gowda's huge moustache, he just couldn't. 'Gowda, I'll not live here. I'll go with my parents,' he said, wiping his tears with the end of the shirt. The Gowda advanced towards him menacingly. 'So, you want to go with your parents? Who will settle the debts then? Why are you worried? The work isn't heavy here. You just look after the cattle and eat as much as you like. Why do you want to go away?' Basava was afraid the Gowda would catch hold of him. 'No, no,' he said, 'I'll not work for you. I'll go with my father. I'll go away from this place.' Basava ran out of the house. The barking dogs followed him for some distance but couldn't catch him. Basava ran fast. He wanted to reach home before the family departed. 'What shall I do, if they have gone?' The question had already left roots in his mind like perennial grass.

Basava stopped in front of his home, and looked at the door. It was not locked; it was open. He concluded that Gowda had lied to him. His only worry now was whether any huggi had been left for him. He was about to cross the threshold when he saw his favourite spotted dog breathing heavily and walking on unsteady legs. He collapsed at Basava's feet and died. Basava patted the dog and tried to talk to him. He didn't see the grains of huggi sticking to the dog's mouth. 'Appa, the dog has died,' he shouted and entered the house.

Translated by G.S. Amur

GLOSSARY

conjee	gruel
huggi	a sweet dish made of split gram, jaggery, and rice
katta	bed consisting of a frame strung with tapes or light rope
mora	winnowing tray

QUESTIONS FOR DISCUSSION

Reading the Story

1. Would you agree that this story is a powerful expression of poverty and hunger? How does this story work for you?
2. This story is written from a child's perspective. How does this shape the narrative?
3. Study the ironic contrast between Basava's joyous anticipation of the sweet dish and his parents' anguish. Do you think that this lends poignancy to the story?
4. Notice how the parents' knowledge of what is to come colours the entire narrative. Did you feel the undercurrent of tension running through the story?

5. Pick out the sentences which you feel speak of the tender relationship that Basava shares with his parents.
6. The evocative use of the title reflects the child's state of mind. What passages describe his expectation of actually eating the sweet? Did you find them effective?
7. It is evident that Basava and his family are at the lowest end of the social ladder. How does this come through in Basava's conversations with other children, the shopkeeper, and Gowda?
8. What did you think of Basava's understanding of the truth? Does he fully grasp all the implications of being sold to Gowda? Or do you think that he would rather not face reality and hopes that he can go back to his old life?
9. The masterly ending of the story deserves close study. Merely hinting at tragedy and leaving things unsaid speak volumes. What did you think?
10. The story works at so many levels and combines many elements. It is powerful and direct, yet sensitive and nuanced. What makes it such a successful short story?

Translation Issues

11. The original title in Kannada is 'Huggi', which the translator has translated as 'A Sweet Dish'. How would you have translated it?
12. The author exhibits masterly control over language, form, and structure. Notice how every sentence is relevant to the story. Has the translator captured all the nuances? Show a few instances.

Activities

13. Pick any sweet dish special to the region you are from and write at least a paragraph on it.
14. Has the plight of any child like Basava ever touched you? Write about your experience.
15. Write a slogan campaigning against child labour in the Indian language you are most familiar with. Translate it into English.

H. NAGAVENI (b. 1962)

H. Nagaveni is from Honnakatte in coastal Karnataka and has two important publications to her credit: *Naakane Neeru* (The Bath on the Fourth Day), an anthology of short stories published in 1997 and *Gandhi Banda* (Gandhi Arrives), a novel published in 1999. Both the books are Sahitya Akademi Award winners. Nagaveni was formerly an Assistant Editor of the Indian National Bibliography at the National Library, Kolkata; she now works as Assistant Librarian at Kannada University, Hampi.

ಸೀಮಂತ

ಸೀತೆ ಅಪ್ಪನೊಂದಿಗೆ ಕಾಲಾವರಕ್ಕೆ ಸೀಮಂತಕ್ಕೆ ಹೊರಟದ್ದಳು, ಅಪ್ಪನ ಬಲ ಕೈ ಹಿಡಿದು ಪುಟ್ಟ ಹೆಜ್ಜೆ ಹಾಕುತ್ತಿದ್ದ ಸೀತೆಯ ಮೈಯಿಡೀ ಸಂಭ್ರಮ ಜಿನುಗುತ್ತಿತ್ತು. ಸೀಮಂತದ 'ವೈಭವ'ನ್ನೊಮ್ಮೆ ಕಣ್ಣಾರೆ ಕಾಣಬೇಕೆಂಬ ಆಸೆ ಆಕೆಗೆ ಬಹಳ ದಿನಗಳಿಂದ. ಇದೀಗ ಸ್ವಂತ ಮಾಮಿಯದೇ ಸೀಮಂತ.

ಸೀತೆ, ಸೀಮಂತ ಎಂಬ ಪದ ಕೇಳಿದ್ದಲ್ಲೇ ಏನಾ ಒಮ್ಮೆಯೂ ಅದರ ಸಂಭ್ರಮ ಸವಿದವಳಲ್ಲ. 'ಒಂದೇ ಒಂದು ಸಲ ನನ್ನನ್ನು ಸೀಮಂತಕ್ಕೆ ಕರೆದೊಯ್ಯಮ್ಮ' - ಎಂದು ಅಮ್ಮನಲ್ಲಿ ಆಕೆ ಅದೆಷ್ಟೋ ಬಾರಿ ಕೊರಳಡ್ಡ ಹಾಕಿ ಗೋಗರೆದಿದ್ದಾಳೆ. 'ನಿನ್ನ ಬಸ್ತಿಯಲ್ಲಿ ನಂಗೆ ಸೀಮಂತ ಮಾಡಿದ್ದು ನೀನು ನೋಡಿಲ್ವೇನ - ಎಂದು ಅಮ್ಮ ಸೀತೆಯ ತಲೆ ಸವರಿ ರಂಗಿನ ಮಾತನಾಡುವಾಗ ಸೀತೆ ಸಿಡುಕುತ್ತಾಳ್ಪಟ್ಟೇ - ಅಸಹನೆಯಿಂದ. ಆ ಮನೆ ಈ ಮನೆಯವರು ಅಲ್ಲಲ್ಲಿ ನಡೆದ ಸೀಮಂತದ ಬಗ್ಗೆ, ಬಸುರಿಗೆ ಬಡಿಸಿದ ಸಿಹಿ ತಿಂಡಿಗಳ ಬಗ್ಗೆ ಬಾಯಿ ಕಿವಿಗಳಲ್ಲಿ ನೀರೂರುವ ಹಾಗೆ, ಮೂರಕ್ಕೆ ನಾಕು ಸೇರಿಸಿ ಹೇಳುವಾಗಲೆಲ್ಲಾ ಸೀತೆ ಆಸೆ ಕುತೂಹಲ ತಡೆಯಲಾರದೆ ಅಮ್ಮನಲ್ಲಿ ಹಲವು ಪ್ರಶ್ನೆಗಳನ್ನು ಕೇಳುವುದಿದೆ.

'ಸೀಮಂತ ಅಂದ್ರೆ ಏನಮ್ಮ?' ಎಂಬುದು ಆಕೆಯ ಮೊದಲ ಪ್ರಶ್ನೆ. 'ಹಾಗಂದ್ರೆ ಬಯಕೆ' ಎಂದು ಅಮ್ಮನೆಂದರೆ, 'ಬಯಕೆ ಅಂದ್ರೇನಮ್ಮ?' ಎಂಬುದು ಮರು ಪ್ರಶ್ನೆ. 'ಬಸುರಿಯರು ಆಸೆ ಪಡುವ ತಿಂಡಿಗಳನ್ನು ತಿನ್ನಿಸುವುದು. ಎಂದು ಅಮ್ಮನೆಂದರೆ 'ಬಸ್ತಿ ಯಾಕಾಗ್ತಾರಮ್ಮ.............ಹೇಗಾಗ್ತಾರೆ'? ಹೀಗೆ ಪ್ರಶ್ನೆಗಳ ಸರಮಾಲೆ ಬೆಳೆಯುತ್ತಿರುತ್ತೆ. ಅಮ್ಮನೂ ತಾಳ್ಮೆಯಿಂದ, ಜಾಣ್ಮೆಯಿಂದ ಉತ್ತರಿಸುತ್ತಾಳೆ. ಅಮ್ಮನ ಉತ್ತರವೆಂದರೆ ಸೀತೆಗೆ ಒಂಥರಾ ತುರಿಗಜ್ಜಿ ಇದ್ದಂತೆ. ತುರಿಸಿದಂತೆಲ್ಲ ಇನ್ನಷ್ಟು ತುರಿಕೆ ಆ ಕಜ್ಜಿ ಸುತ್ತಲೇ ಹುಟ್ಟಿಕೊಳ್ಳುವಂತೆ, ಅಮ್ಮ ಉತ್ತರಿಸಿದಂತೆಲ್ಲ ಮತ್ತೆ ಮತ್ತೇ ಉತ್ತರದ ಸುತ್ತ ಇನ್ನಷ್ಟು ಪ್ರಶ್ನೆಗಳು ಹುಟ್ಟಿಕೊಳ್ಳುತ್ತಿದ್ದವು. ಅಮ್ಮನ ತಾಳ್ಮೆಯ ಕುಡಿಕೆ ಬರಿದಾಗುವುದು- 'ನಾನು ಬಸಿರಾಗುವುದು ಯಾವಾಗಮ್ಮ, ನಂಗೂ ಸೀಮಂತ ಮಾಡ್ತಿಯಾ' ಎಂಬ ಪ್ರಶ್ನೆಯನ್ನು ಸೀತೆ ಅಮ್ಮನತ್ತ ಎಸೆದಾಗ ಮಾತ್ರ.

'ಬಾಯ್ಮುಚ್ಚಿ ದಿಂಡೆ ಬಸವಿ'- ಎಂದು ತಾಯಿ ಗದರಿಸಿ ತಲೆಗೊಂದು ಮೊಟಕಿದರೆ.

Seemantha[*]

Sita was all ready to leave for Kalavara with her father to attend the *seemantha* ceremony. As she walked, holding her father's right hand, excitement overflowed her little steps. How long she had waited to watch the grandeur of a seemantha! Now it was her own aunt's seemantha and she could watch it for as long as she wanted.

Sita had only heard the word seemantha, she had never experienced its luxurious excitement. 'Just once, Amma, please take me to a seemantha,' she had cried and pleaded with her mother so many times 'Did you not see the seemantha ceremony arranged for me when I was carrying you?' Amma would lay her hand on Sita's head teasingly and fondle her, annoying Sita. Whenever this or that neighbour referred to a seemantha here or there and mentioned a variety of sweets served for the pregnant woman, it made not just the mouth water but also the ear. Sita could not contain her curiosity and would ask mother a number of questions.

'Amma, what is seemantha?' was her first question. When mother said, 'Seemantha is desire'. 'What is desire?' was Sita's second question. Mother replied, 'To offer the pregnant woman the kind of food she wishes to eat'. 'Why will they become pregnant? How will they become pregnant ...?' The chain of questions increased. Mother too answered Sita with great patience and tact. For Sita, mother's answers were like an eczema. Just as scratching increased the itch, questions sprouted around every reply her mother gave her. Mother's patience was tested when Sita asked, 'Amma, when will I become pregnant? Then, will you arrange a seemantha for me as well?' 'Stop that! You naughty girl!' A smack on her head! Sita would fall silent just for that moment. But once a child is curious, will her curiosity ever wane? That little mind was dying to know more and more about

---

[*]Seemantha

pregnancy and Seemantha . It was nothing but the pull of the thread of desire of her tender heart to just once eat the sweets served to the pregnant woman!

Sita was now seated in the Miskith Motor and crossing Udyavara Bridge. For just a moment, the white cranes in the *kandla* bushes on the riverside diverted her attention from her aunt's seemantha. But after a bit, again the thoughts of the seemantha ceremony described by Revathi, especially the boiled egg episode, rushed into her mind! Sita's friend Revathi had recently attended her aunt's seemantha at Bajpe. The very next day she had brought rava laddu and sugar-coated groundnuts to school. She had described at length how her aunt had been dressed like a bride and how she was served innumerable varieties of eatables in the *gerase*. The aunt was seated ceremoniously and in the large tray placed before her, they had served *rava laddu*, *mohan laddu*, *aralude*, *sukrude*, *holige*, sugar-coated groundnuts, *chikkuli*, *maalpuri*, *halwa*, *mithayee*, *jalebi*, boiled eggs ... and many more things. She had described how her aunt had chosen her and her brother amongst the crowd to offer them boiled eggs. Revathi had gone on. Meanwhile, Sita had been so upset that she had thrown the rava laddu out of the window.

She was angry because Revathi had brought rava laddu and not boiled eggs. Sita certainly loved sweets, but her first preference was for boiled eggs. Not even once had she eaten a whole boiled egg. Sita had an insistent desire to eat boiled eggs. Whenever she had demanded it, mother had frowned at her saying, 'Are we great landlords with a thousand *mudi* of land to eat eggs every day?' and hushed her up. She even knew that it was Chakana Seena who boiled the eggs that were displayed at Rampa's toddy shop. Every time she saw them, she wanted to ask mother to buy one for her. But the scolding she received stopped her from asking again.

Sita's mind which had relished Revathi's description of her aunt's seemantha, now turned towards Janaki's seemantha soon to take place at Kalavara. 'When will I reach Kalavara? When will I go and hug Janaki Mami?' the excited Sita endlessly pondered. 'When Mami is served all those exclusive dishes, she will make me stand right next to her. She will give me the boiled eggs and sweets first.' Sita could not decide what to eat and what not to. ... As her calculations ran on, she suddenly remembered her mother's warning.

In the morning when Sita was getting ready to leave for her aunt's seemantha, mother had put a string of beads around her neck and told her, 'My child, talk to Mami only if she talks to you. Don't go on talking like a chatterbox. If they give you something to eat, first refuse. Say no. If you grab it, they will think that you have not eaten for four days. They know we are poor.' She had told Sita many such things. Sita had nodded, saying 'Umm' for everything. Now when she was wondering whether to follow mother's instructions or simply let them out of the window, her father's thoughts took a different turn altogether.

Sita's father was Gopala Ganiga. When his parents died, he had taken the responsibility of his two grown up younger sisters and brought them from the village to his house. He had sold his wife's jewellery and taken loans from nearly everyone to get Sumathi, the elder one, married to Keshava, son of Dabbu Ganiga from Jokatte. The second one was Janaki. By the time she too was settled, he was ruined. Gopala who worked in the godown at Kinningoli was already an asthma patient. Half his salary was spent on his treatment and the other half on managing the house and sundry expenses. In such a poverty-stricken situation, the sister's marriage had been a real burden for Gopala. When, unexpectedly, Sumathi's husband Keshava brought a marriage proposal from a very rich family for Janaki to be a second wife, Gopala accepted it without any hesitation. Janaki, who did not want to be a second wife, accepted it half-heartedly with a woebegone face. The prosperity and prestige of her husband's house cooled her anger a bit and brought her woebegone face back to normal. Janaki was soon swimming in so much milk and honey that she did not spare a single thought for her people. It was now the *Suggi* month. By the next month, that is *Bhesha*, it would be one year since Janaki's marriage. During the last *Aati* month, Gopala had visited his sister's place to invite her home. She had refused to go with him. After that he had also not bothered to visit her. So this was the second time he was visiting Janaki's house. While Gopala Ganiga sat thinking about his sister's post-delivery expenses, hundreds of ideas were rushing through little Sita's mind. The ceremony, the boiled eggs, aunt Janaki's house, the heaps of sweets, all these competed with one another for her attention.

Gopala entered the courtyard with Sita. Sita who was astonished to see the two-storied house, thought that her aunt's house was also as big as Revathi's. As they crossed the courtyard and approached the verandah, her aunt Janaki's husband received them. Sita's eyes searched for her aunt, who was nowhere to be seen. She sat with her father in a corner in the verandah, and pestered him for her aunt. 'She will come now, she will be here any time,' he tried to convince her.

Gradually Sita's attention shifted from her aunt to the women who sat in the inner hall. Women in zari saris, decked in gold ornaments, sat chatting. Awed, Sita looked at them wide-eyed. All her attention was now on the woman in a red zari sari. Her neck loaded with gold necklaces reminded Sita of the neck of the ox that pulled Esmail Berry's cart. She wanted to whisper this at once to her father. Already feeling uncomfortable and anxious to see his sister, Gopala's eyes searched for her all over the house. Sita noticed him looking around and decided to keep quiet.

Once again she remembered her aunt. A strange fear stopped her from entering the inner hall. The huge carved doors, neatly upholstered furniture, and smooth clean slippery floor! She was scared even to move her feet beyond where she sat. On top of this … her mother's warning! She continued to sit silently.

Sita's attention was on the inner room. Every now and then, as she thought of her aunt, the thought of the boiled eggs also surfaced. She thought of Revathi as well. When Sita was looking in some other direction, her aunt appeared. Abbah! Gopala felt relieved.

Sita was excited to see her aunt. 'I'll go touch Mami just once and run back, shall I?' she asked her father quietly. 'No, she will come here and hug you,' he said. Sita waited and waited. Aunt Janaki did not look like she would come Sita's way. She was busy smiling and talking to those women in zari saris in the inner hall.

Gopala also felt a bit awkward. Why was Janaki not coming this way? Sita's anguish and impatience increased. When she asked repeatedly if she could go in, Gopala agreed.

Sita ran towards her aunt and hugged her. 'When did you come? Where is appa?' asked Janaki, her face expressionless. Sita pointed towards her father. Janaki threw a wry smile at her brother, said, 'I'll be back now,' moved away from Sita, and went inside.

Sita felt humiliated. Father had told her, 'Mami will hug you, hold you close and cuddle you.' She neither hugged her nor shoved her off. She just removed Sita's arms from around her and moved away. Sita could not bear this. She came running to her father, hid her face in his lap, and wept. Gopala sighed helplessly.

Gopala was trying to console his daughter. 'Mami went indoors to dress like a bride. She will wear a zari sari, the flat round golden flower on her head, lots of gold jewellery. Then she will come to you, hug you, and be photographed with you. ...' Gopala went on saying so many things but Sita was not convinced.

Meanwhile, Gopala's other sister Sumathi arrived with her husband and daughter. As soon as she saw her brother, she came towards them and hugged Sita.

Sita was diverted by aunt Sumathi's daughter, Sharada. Both girls started playing. Gopala consulted Sumathi on whether to take Janaki home for her delivery. 'You better keep away from this. Why do you want to get into trouble? People like you cannot afford to take the responsibility of the wealthy. Do not ask Janaki and get insulted,' she advised him. Gopala kept quiet.

Meanwhile, Janaki's sisters-in-law led the gorgeously dressed Janaki to the hall. 'Chikkamma,' called out Sharada in a loud voice. Janaki did not hear her. Sumathi frowned at her daughter and signaled her to shut up.

It was only Sumathi's and Gopala's families that attended the seemantha ceremony from Janaki's side. This did not make any difference to Janaki nor did she feel bad about it. Janaki's sisters-in-law led her to a chair and placed a three-legged table before her. On the table was the tray in which they began serving dishes for her. Baskets full of sweets, one after the other were carried out. As the aroma of the sweets reached them, Sita and Sharada stopped playing and ran towards the womenfolk who surrounded Janaki. Sumathi ran and caught hold of her daughter, but Sita slipped out and escaped. She went and stood right next to Janaki.

Sita looked at her ornaments without blinking an eyelid. She felt that her aunt was more beautiful than Bhagirathi teacher. When Sita saw the different kinds of jewellery her aunt was wearing, she was reminded of her mother's bare wrists and neck.

Her aunt's husband stood beside her and was directing where and how the sweets should be served. When Sita looked at him and then at the sparkling rings on his fingers, she forgot both the sweets and her aunt for a while. Suddenly Sita remembered the boiled eggs. She remembered how the boiled eggs were served to Revathi's aunt at her seemantha and how she had given them to Revathi.

Boiled eggs had not yet been served to aunt. Sita was waiting for them. Aunt's gerase was full of sweets of various shapes, names, sizes and colours. Till then she had never seen such things nor had she heard about them. Why Sita! Even Kamath of the bakery might not have seen them. Sita's mouth watered on seeing such exotic sweets that decorated aunt's tray and she wanted to eat at least a little from each variety. As this went on, she was also anxious about those eggs. No one was serving aunt eggs! Sita craned her neck and looked around. There were no boiled eggs in any of the baskets or bowls. Everyone was serving aunt only sweets. Sita's patience began to run dry. Thinking someone might bring eggs, she peeped around. No sign of any. None of them even mentioned eggs. Aunt could not see those standing in front of her as the heap of sweets blocked her vision. This heap of sweets was passed over Sita's head.

Then it was the turn of fruit. Sita's tension rose. Boiled eggs had not come yet! 'Get boiled eggs after fruit,' aunt's husband gave instructions to his brother-in-law. 'Abbah! At last!' thought Sita.

Sita's excitement began to flow again. The serving of fruit was also over. Boiled eggs were the only things left now. Sita inched towards her aunt. The person who had gone indoors to get them had not yet returned. Sita was so angry that she felt like biting him. 'Who's there, get the eggs!' Aunt's husband roared and hastily the peeled boiled eggs appeared.

Aunt's husband seemed a very nice person to Sita. When she witnessed that his orders resulted in the instant appearance of boiled eggs, she thought he must be more powerful than her schoolmaster.

Finally, aunt was served boiled eggs. Sita's mouth watered as she watched them. Aunt's husband who was all smiles was forcing her to eat. People around aunt also forced her to eat. Aunt was not eating. She was feeling shy! 'Arre!! What happened to this mami? When she was in our house she would grab it at once and gulp it down,' Sita was surprised. Again aunt's husband was forcing her to eat and he put a piece of halwa into her mouth. People sitting around laughed. Sita also laughed.

Janaki ate a few pieces of halwa and now stretched her hand towards the boiled eggs. Sita could hear her heart begin to thud! 'Give the eggs to two children you like the most,' said aunt's eldest sister-in-law in a low voice. Aunt started looking at the children around her. To establish her presence, Sita inched towards her aunt and stood leaning on her.

Janaki's search continued. 'Let Mami look at me at least once,' wished Sita. Janaki looked straight down her nose and did not bother to look to either side. She took an egg from the gerase, placed it in the hands of the child the red zari sari woman was carrying. That child was busy looking elsewhere. As the egg fell into her hand, the child's disgust came out in the form of a loud '!! ii ... shh ... ee!' and she threw the egg back at Janaki. 'She hates eggs and you have given it to her,' laughed the child's mother loudly, her mouth open as wide as the town. Janaki also joined in her laughter but sounded confused and silly.

The egg, which the child threw, was about to fall on Janaki but missed her and fell on Sita who was standing next to her. For a moment, Sita was embarrassed. Somewhere within her she also felt happy because Janaki turned to see where the egg had fallen and she was standing right there! Since the egg had fallen on Sita, everyone's attention was focused on her. Sita was happy that at least now her aunt had noticed her. She was also very angry with the child who had thrown the egg. 'Why should she throw it? If she did not want she could have returned it,' thought Sita. On the one hand she was very angry, on the other she was eager to know to whom aunt would give the other egg.

Again aunt picked up another boiled egg. For a moment her gaze fell on Sita standing next to her, and then slowly it moved in some other direction. Sita thought, 'Is she holding the egg and chanting some mantras like Manku Josia who lives in the opposite house?' Aunt turned again towards Sita. Sita was excited! Aunt would give her the egg! She was thrilled!

Janaki called her sister-in-law's daughter who was standing far away. Though the girl did not want the egg she forced her to eat it. Aunt fed her personally.

Sita who stood like an embodiment of desire suddenly stepped on the boiled egg lying at her feet and smashed it. She could not take the grandeur of the seemantha any more. She ran back to her father and hid her face in his lap. 'Child, did you see the seemantha?' he asked, caressing her cheek.

Translated by Mamta Sagar

GLOSSARY

Aati	A girl is expected to stay away from her in-law's house during the first Aashada of her married life. It is a custom for the girl's brother to bring her back home for this period.
chikkamma	aunt younger than one's parents
gerase	A tray made of bamboo, used to separate rice from husk, stones, dust, and insects
mami	maternal aunt
mudi	measure of land
rava laddu, mohan laddu, araludu, sukrude, holige, sugar-coated groundnuts, chikkuli, maalpuri, halwa, mithayee, jalebi	sweets and savouries usually made for ceremonial occasions
sanyasi	a spiritual seeker who has renounced the world
seemantha	ceremony performed during the eighth month of the first pregnancy in the husband's house
zari	gold thread

QUESTIONS FOR DISCUSSION

Reading the Story

1. What emotions did you experience when you read the story? Elaborate.
2. The story is written from the third-person point of view which delves into the mind of a child. Does this make the story all the more poignant and effective?
3. A child's perspective on life is both naive and refreshingly different. For instance, a child notices details that would escape an adult. Pick out examples from the text.
4. Would you agree that it is more challenging to write from a child's point of view? Why?

5. The story speaks of the power of money. How does the author successfully convey this to the reader?
6. The stories 'Taatayya' and 'A Sweet Dish' also have children as protagonists. Compare 'Seemantha' with these stories.
7. Sita's longing for her favourite food, a boiled egg, is partly an expression of her deeply felt need for love and attention. Would you agree?

Translation Issues

8. How is it immediately apparent that this story is a translation?
9. The translator has made conscious decisions to retain certain culture-specific terms in the story. Is she justified in doing so? Pick out examples.

Activities

10. How do you think Sita herself would have told the story? Write the story from her point of view using the first person.
11. Ask any of the elders in your family to recount an incident around a ritual from their childhood. Translate it into English keeping in mind the ethnographic details.
12. Pick out a story written from a child's perspective in any of the Indian languages you know best. Translate the most interesting paragraph.

A.K. Ramanujan (1929–93)

An award-winning translator, poet, essayist, folklorist, and scholar, A.K. Ramanujan has been widely published and anthologized. Born into a Tamil family in Mysore, he studied at the University of Mysore and at Indiana University. He taught at the University of Chicago and generations of scholars, writers, and translators owe much to him. Ramanujan translated from Tamil and medieval Kannada. His translations of Sangam poetry are widely admired. He also wrote poetry in English and experimental verse in Kannada. He gathered folktales from all over India. He was a bilingual writer and a translator who moved with great ease between three languages—English, Tamil, and Kannada. He was awarded the Padma Shri in 1976. He also won a posthumous prize from the Sahitya Akademi for poetry in English. His works include *The Striders, Interior Landscapes: Love Poems from a Classical Tamil Anthology, Relations, Speaking of Siva, Hymns for the Drowning, The Epic of Palnadu: A Study of Translation of Palnati Vinula Katha, A Telugu Oral Tradition from Andhra Pradesh, India, Poems of Love and War, Second Sight, Another Harmony: New Essays on the Folklore of India, Folktales from India, Oral Tales from Twenty Indian Languages,* and *A Flowering Tree and Other Oral Tales from India.* He co-edited *The Oxford Anthology of Modern Indian Poetry* with Vinay Dharwadker.

ಅಣ್ಣಯ್ಯನ ಮಾನವಶಾಸ್ತ್ರ ★ ಎ.ಕೆ. ರಾಮಾನುಜನ್

ಆವನಿಗೆ ಆಶ್ಚರ್ಯ, ಬಹಳ ಆಶ್ಚರ್ಯ

ಈ ಅಮೆರಿಕಾದ ಮಾನವಶಾಸ್ತ್ರಿ, ಈ ಫರ್ಗುಸನ್ ನೋಡಿ. ಮನು ಓದಿದಾನೆ. ಇವನಿಗೆ ನಮ್ಮ ಸೂತಕಗಳ ಬಗ್ಗೆ ಎಷ್ಟು ವಿಷಯ ಗೊತ್ತಿದೆ! ತಾನು ಬ್ರಾಹ್ಮಣ. ತನಗೇ ಇದೆಲ್ಲ ಗೊತ್ತಿಲ್ಲ.

ಅಮೆರಿಕಕ್ಕೆ ಬರಬೇಕು ಆತ್ಮಜ್ಞಾನಕ್ಕೆ. ಮಹಾತ್ಮಾರು ಜೈಲಿನಲ್ಲಿ ಕೂತು ಕಂಬಿ ಮಧ್ಯ ಆತ್ಮಚರಿತ್ರೆ ಬರೆದ ಹಾಗೆ. ನೆಹರು ಇಂಗ್ಲೆಂಡಿಗೆ ಹೋಗಿ ಸ್ವದೇಶ ಕಂಡುಕೊಂಡ ಹಾಗೆ. ದೂರದಲ್ಲಿದ್ದರೇ ಬೆಟ್ಟ

ನಮ್ಮ ದೇಹದ ಹನ್ನೆರಡು ದ್ರವಗಳಿಂದ ನಮಗೆ ಮಲದ ಸೋಂಕು :

ದೇಹದ ಜಿಡ್ಡುಗಳು, ವೀರ್ಯ, ರಕ್ತ ಮಿದುಳಿನ ಮಜ್ಜೆಯ ನೀರು, ಮೂತ್ರ, ಹೇಲು, ಶಿಂಬಳ, ಕಿವಿಯ ಕಿಸುರು, ಕಫ, ಕಣ್ಣೀರು, ಕಣ್ಣಿನ ಪಿಸುರ್, ಮೈಚರ್ಮದ ಬೆವರು

(ಮನು 5.135)

ಚಿಕಾಗೋವಿನಲ್ಲಿದ್ದರೂ ಎಣಿಸುವುದು ಕನ್ನಡದಲ್ಲೇ. ಎಣಿಸಿದ ಒಂದು ಎರಡು ಮೂರು ನಾಲ್ಕು ಐದು ಆರು ಏಳು ಎಂಟು ಒಂಭತ್ತು ಹತ್ತು ಹನ್ನೊಂದು. ಹನ್ನೊಂದು, ಮೊದಲನೇ ಸಾರಿ ಎಣಿಸಿದಾಗ ಹನ್ನೊಂದೆ ಮಲ ಸಿಕ್ತಿತ. ಮತ್ತೆ ಎಣಿಸಿದಾಗ, ಹನ್ನೆರಡು. ಸರಿಯಾಗಿ ಹನ್ನೆರಡು. ಆವನಿಗೆ ಗೊತ್ತಿದ್ದ ಈ ಹನ್ನೆರಡರಲ್ಲಿ ಎಂಜಲು, ಒಂದ, ಎರಡ. ಚಿಕ್ಕಂದಿನಿಂದ ಹೇಳಿದ್ದರು. ಎಂಜಲು ಮಾಡಬಾರದು. ಕಕ್ಕಸ ಮಾಡಿದರೆ ಸರಿಯಾಗಿ ತೊಳೆದುಕೊಳ್ಳಬೇಕು. ಸುಸ್ಸು ಮಾಡಿದರೆ ತೊಳೆಯಬೇಕು. ಆವರತ್ತ ಕಕ್ಕಸಿಗೆ ಹೋದರೆ ಓಡಿಮಣ್ಣು ಮೃತ್ತಿಕೆ ಕೂಡ ತೆಗೆದುಕೊಂಡು ಹೋಗುತ್ತಿದ್ದರು. ಆವರಿರುವವರೆಗೆ ಹೊತ್ತಲ್ಲಿ ಒಂದು ಮಣ್ಣಾ ಗುಳಿ ಯಾವಾಗಲೂ.

ದಕ್ಷಿಣ ದೇಶದಲ್ಲಿ ಬಾಯಿಗಿಟ್ಟು ಎಂಜಲು ಮಾಡಿ ಊದುವ ಪೀಪಿ ನಾಗಸ್ವರಗಳೆಲ್ಲ ಮುಟ್ಟಬಾರದ ವಸ್ತು, ಎಂಜಲು - ಮುಟ್ಟಬಾರದ ಅಸ್ಪಶ್ಯರು ಮಾತ್ರ ಮುಟ್ಟಿ ಬಾರಿಸತಕ್ಕ ವಾದ್ಯ, ವೀಣ ಬ್ರಾಹ್ಮಣಂಗಿಗೆ, ಮುಖವೀಣೆ ಹೊಲ ಜಾತಿಗೆ.

ಮಡಕೆಗಿಂತ ಬೆಳ್ಳಿ; ಹತ್ತಿಗಿಂತ ರೇಷ್ಮೆ ಉತ್ತಮ. ಕಾರಣ, ಅದಕ್ಕೆ ಈ ಹನ್ನೆರಡು ಮಲ ಆಷ್ಟು ಸುಲಭವಾಗಿ ಅಂಟುವುದಿಲ್ಲ. ರೇಷ್ಮೆಯೆ ರೇಶಿಮೆ ಹುಳದ ಮೈಯ ಮಲ ನಿಜ. ಆದರೆ ಅದು ಮನುಷ್ಯರಿಗೆ ಮಡಿ. ನೋಡಿ ಹೇಗಿದೆ.

ಈ ಅಮೆರಿಕನ್ನರಿಗೆ ಎಷ್ಟು ವಿಷಯ ಗೊತ್ತಿದೆ! ಯಾವ ಯಾವದೋ ಲೈಬ್ರರಿಗಳಿಗೆ ಹೋಗಿ ನೋಡಿದ್ದಾರೆ. ಎಂಥೆಂಥ ಕಾಶಿ ಗೊದ್ದು ಪಂಡಿತರ ಕಾಲಜ ಹಿಂಡಿ ಪಾಂಡಿತ್ಯದ ರಸ ಇಳಿಸಿದ್ದಾರೆ. ಎಲ್ಲೆಲ್ಲಿನ ಓಲೆಗರಿ ಹಸ್ತಪ್ರತಿಗಳ ಧೂಳುಹೊಡೆದು ವಸ್ತು ಸಂಗ್ರಹಿಸಿದ್ದಾರೆ. ಆಶ್ಚರ್ಯ, ಪರಮಾಶ್ಚರ್ಯ ಇವನಿಗೆ.

ಹಿಂದ ದೇಶದ ವಿಷಯ ಕಲಿಯಬೇಕಾದರೆ ಫಿಲಡೆಲ್ಫಿಯ, ಬರ್ಕ್ಲೀ, ಚಿಕಾಗೋ, ಅಂಥ ಜಾಗಕ್ಕೆ ಬರಬೇಕು. ನಮಗೆಲ್ಲಿ ಇವರ ಆಸ್ಥೆ? ವಿವೇಕಾನಂದರು ಕೂಡ ಚಿಕಾಗೋವಿಗೆ ಬರಲಿಲ್ಲವೆ? ಆವರು ನಮ್ಮ ಧರ್ಮದ ಮೇಲ ಕೊಟ್ಟ ಮೊದಲ ಭಾಷಣ ಇಲ್ಲ.

ಸೂತಕ ತರುವ ಮೂರು ಜೀವ ಕ್ರಿಯೆಗಳಲ್ಲಿ ಮುಟ್ಟಾಗುವುದು ಮೊದಲು, ಹುಟ್ಟುವುದು ಅದಕ್ಕಿಂತ ಒಂದು ಡಿಗ್ರಿ ಹೆಚ್ಚಿನದು. ಎಲ್ಲಕ್ಕಿಂತ ಬಲವತ್ತರವಾದ ಸೂತಕ ಸಾವಿನ ಸೂತಕ. ಸಾವಿನ ಸೋಂಕಿದ್ದರೆ ಸಾಕು: ಏನೂ ಸೂತಕ ತರುತ್ತದೆ. ಉರಿಯುವ ಚಟ್ಟದ ಹೊಗೆ ಸೋಕಿದರೆ ಸಾಕು ಬ್ರಾಹ್ಮಣ ಸ್ನಾನ ಮಾಡಬೇಕು. ಹೊಲೆಯರಲ್ಲದೆ ಮಿಕ್ಕವರಾರೂ ಸತ್ತವನುಟ್ಟ ಬಟ್ಟೆ ಉಡುವ ಹಾಗಿಲ್ಲ.

(ಮನು 10.39)

ಶುಭದಲ್ಲಿ ಶುಭವಾದ ಹಸು ಸತ್ತರೆ ಆದರ ದೇಹದ ಮಾಂಸ ತಿನ್ನುವವರು ಎಲ್ಲರಿಗಿಂತ ಕೀಳುಜಾತಿ : ಕಾಗೆ ಹದ್ದು ಕೂಡ ಈ ಕಾರಣಕ್ಕೆ ಹಕ್ಕಿ ಜಾತಿಯಲ್ಲಿ 'ಕೀಳು ಹಕ್ಕಿ. ಕೆಲವು ಸಾರಿ ಸಾವಿಗೂ ಅಸ್ಪಶ್ಯತೆಗೂ ಇರುವ ಅಂಟು

Annayya's Anthropology[*]

Annayya couldn't help but marvel at the American anthropologist. 'Look at this Fergusson,' he thought, 'he has not only read Manu, our ancient law-giver, but knows all about our ritual pollutions. Here I am, a Brahmin myself, yet I don't know a thing about such things.'

You want self-knowledge? You should come to America. Just as the Mahatma had to go to jail and sit behind bars to write his autobiography. Or as Nehru had to go to England to discover India. Things are clear only when looked at from a distance.

Oily exudations, semen, blood, the fatty substance of the brain, urine, faeces, the mucus of the nose, ear wax, phlegm, tears, the rheum of the eyes, and sweat are the twelve impurities of human bodies.

(Manu 5: 135)

He counted. Though he had been living in Chicago for years, he still counted in Kannada. One, two, three, four, five, six, seven, eight, nine, ten, eleven ... eleven ... eleven ... At first he could count only eleven body wastes. When he counted again, he counted twelve. Yes, exactly twelve. Of these twelve, he already knew about spittle, urine, and faeces. He had been told as a child not to spit, to clean himself after a bowel movement and after urinating. Whenever his aunt went to the outhouse, she took with her a handful of clay. She cleaned herself with a pinch of clay. As long as she lived, there used to be a clay pit in the backyard.

In the southern regions of the country, wind instruments like the *nagaswara* were considered unclean because they came in contact with the player's spittle. And so, only Untouchables could touch or play them. Thus, the *vina,* the stringed instrument, was for the Brahmins; and the rest, the wind instruments, were for the low castes.

---

[*]Annayana Manavashastra

Silverware is cleaner than earthernware; silk is purer than cotton. The reason was that they are not easily tainted by the twelve kinds of body-wastes. Silk, which is the bodily secretion of the silkworm, is nonetheless pure for human beings. Think of that!

What a lot of things these Americans know! Whether it means wearing out the steps of libraries or sitting at the feet of saucy pundits, or blowing the dust off old palm-leaf manuscripts, they spare no effort in collecting their materials and distilling the essence of scholarship. Annayya found all this amazing. Simply amazing!

If you want to learn things about India, you should come to places like Philadelphia, Berkeley, Chicago. Where in India do we have such dedication to learning? Even Swami Vivekananda came to Chicago, didn't he? And it is here that he made his first speech on our religion.

Of the three kinds of bodily functions that bring impurity, the first one is menstruation. Parturition/childbirth causes a higher degree of impurity. The highest and the most severe impurity is, of course, on account of death. Even the slightest contact with death will bring some impurity. Even if the smoke from a cremation fire touches a Brahmin, he has to take a bath and purify himself. No one, except the lowest caste *holeya,* can wear the clothes removed from the dead body.

(Manu 10: 39)

The cow being the most sacred of all animals, only people of the lowest of the castes eat the flesh of the cow's cadaver. For this very reason, the crow and the scavenger kite are considered the lowest among birds. The relationship between death and Untouchability is sometimes very subtle. In Bengal, for instance, there are two subcastes of people in the oil profession: those who only sell oil are of a higher caste, whereas those who actually work the oilpress are of a lower caste. The reason is that the latter destroy life by crushing the oil-seeds and therefore are contaminated by death.

(Hutton 1946: 77–8)

He had known none of this.

Not that he hadn't read a lot. Many a pair of sandals had he worn out walking every day to and from the University library in Mysore. The five or six library clerks there were all known to him. Especially Shetty, who had sat with him in the economics class. He had failed the previous year, and he had taken the library job. Whenever Annayya went to the library, Shetty would hand him the whole bunch of keys to the stacks so that Annayya could open any bookcase and look for whatever book he wanted.

The bunch of keys was heavy because of the many keys in it. There were the iron keys which, with much handling, had become smooth and shiny. Ensconced amidst them were tiny, bright, brass keys. Brass keys for brass locks. Male keys for female locks. Female keys for male locks. Big keys for the big locks. Small keys for the small locks. And there were also a few small keys for big locks and some big keys for small locks. So many combinations like the varieties of marriage which Manu talks about in his book. Some locks were simply too big for their cupboards and so they were left unlocked. Others were nearly impossible to unlock. You would have to break open the cupboard if you wanted to get at the one book that beckoned you tantalizingly. Who knew what social-science-related nude pictures that one book contained!

When he was in Mysore, much of what he read had to do with Western subjects, and they were almost always in English. If he read anything at all in Kannada, rare as it was, it would probably be a translation of Anna Karenina or a book on Shakespeare by Murthy Rao, or ethnographic studies done by scholars who were trained overseas in America. But, now, he himself was in America.

The knowledge of Brahmin austerities, fire, holy food, earth, restraint of the internal organs, water, smearing with cow dung, the wind, sacred rites, the sun, and time are the purifiers of corporeal beings.

(Manu 5: 105)

To learn about these things, Annayya, himself the son of Annayya Shrotry, after crossing 10,000 miles and many waters, lands, and climes, had to come to this cold, stinking Chicago. How did these white men learn all our dark secrets? Who whispered the sacred chants into their ears? Take, for instance, Max Mueller of Germany who had mastered Sanskrit so well that he came to be known among Indian pundits as '*Moksha Mula Bhatta*'. He, in turn, taught the Vedas to the Indians themselves!

When he lived in India, Annayya was obsessed with things American, English, or European. Once here in America, he began reading more and more about India; began talking more and more about India to anyone who would listen. Made the Americans drink his coffee; drank their beer with them. Talked about palmistry and held the hands of white women while pretending to read their palms.

Annayya pursued anthropology like a lecher pursuing the object of his desire—with no fear, no shame, as they say in Sanskrit. He became obsessed with the desire to know everything about his Indian tradition; read any anthropological work on the subject which he could lay his hands on. On the second floor of the Chicago library were stacks and stacks of those books which had to be reached by climbing the ladders and holding on to the wooden railings. Library call number PK 321. The East had at last found itself a niche in the West.

'Why do your women wear that red dot on their foreheads?' the white girls he befriended at the International House would ask him. He had to read and search in order to satisfy their curiosity. He read the Gita. In Mysore, he had made his father angry by refusing to read it. Here he drank beer and whisky, ate beef, used toilet paper instead of washing himself with water, lapped up the Playboy magazines with their pictures of naked breasts, thighs, and some navels as big as rupee coins. But in the midst of all that, he found time to read. He read about the Hindu tradition when he should have been reading economics, he found time to prepare a list of books published by the Ramakrishna Mission while working on mathematics and statistics. 'This is where you come, to America, if you want to learn about Hindu civilization,' he thought to himself. He found himself saying to fellow Indians, 'Do you know that our library in Chicago gets even Kannada newspapers, even *Prajawani*?' He had found the key, the American key, to open the many closed doors of Hindu civilization. He had found the entire bunch of keys.

That day, while browsing in the Chicago stacks, he chanced upon a new book, a thick one with a blue hardcover. Written on the spine in golden letters was the title: *Hinduism: Custom and Ritual*. Author, Steven Fergusson. Published quite recently. The information gathered in it was all fresh. Dozens of rituals and ceremonies: ceremony for a woman's first pregnancy, ceremonies for naming a child, for cutting the child's hair for the first time, for feeding the child solid food for the first time, for wearing the sacred thread, the marriage vows taken while walking the seven steps, the partaking of fruit and almond milk by the

newly-weds on their wedding night.(He remembered someone
making a lewd joke: 'Do you know what the chap is going to do on his
wedding night? He is going to ply his bride with cardamoms and
almonds, and he himself will drink almond milk in preparation for
you know what!') The Sanskrit chant on love-making which the
husband recites to his wife. The ritual celebrating a man's sixtieth
birthday. Rituals for propitiation, for giving charity, purification rituals,
obsequial rituals, and so on. Everything was explained in great detail
in this book.

Page 163. A detailed description of the cremation rites among
Brahmins with illustrations. What an amazing information this
Fergusson chap had given! There was a quotation from Manu on every
page. The formulae for offering sacrifices to the ancestors: which
ancestral line can be considered your own and which not. The
impurity that comes from death does not affect a sanyasi and a baby
that hasn't started teething yet. If a baby dies after teething, the impurity
resulting from it lasts for one day; if it is from the death of a child who
has had his first haircutting ceremony, the impurity is for three days.
The rituals concerning a death anniversary involve seven generations:
the son, the grandson, and his son who perform the death anniversary;
the father, the grandfather, and the great-grandfather for whom the
anniversary is performed. Three generations above, three generations
below, yourself in the middle. The book was crammed with such
details. It even had a table that listed the number of days to show how
different castes are affected by death-related impurities. Moreover, if a
patrilineal relative dies in a distant land, you are not subject to the
impurity as long as you have not heard the news of the death. But the
impurity begins as soon as you have heard the news. You have to then
calculate the number of days of impurity accordingly and at the end
take the bath of purification. The more Annayya read on through the
book, the more fascinated he became.

Sitting between two stacks, he went on reading the book. All the
four aspects of the funeral rites were explained in it. All these years,
Annayya had not really seen a death. Once or twice, he had seen the
people of the washerman's caste, a few streets from his own in a
procession with the dead body of a relative all decked up. That was the
closest he had ever come to witnessing a death. When his uncle died,
Annayya was away in Bombay. When he left for America, his father was

suffering from a mild form of diabetes. But the doctor had assured him it was not life-threatening as long as his father was careful with his diet. His father had suffered a stroke a year-and-a-half ago. It had left his hands and the left side of his face paralysed. Still, he was all right, according to the letters his mother routinely wrote in a shaky hand once every two weeks. In her letters, she would keep reminding him that every Saturday he should massage himself with oil before his bath or else he would suffer from excessive heat. In cold countries, you have to be careful about body heat. Would he like her to send him some soap-nut for his oil baths?

When a Brahmin is nearing his death, he is lifted up from the bed and is placed on a layer of sacred grass spread on the floor, his feet facing south. The bed or the cot prevents the dying person's body from remaining in contact with the elemental earth and the sky. The grass, however, is part of the elements, having drawn its sap from the earth. It is dear to the fire. South is the direction of Yama, the God of Death; it is also the direction of the ancestral world.

Next , the Vedic chants are uttered in the dying person's ear and *panchagavya*—a sacred mixture made of cow's milk, curds, ghee, urine, and dung—is poured into his mouth. A dead human being is unclean. But the urine and dung of a living cow are purifying. Think of that!

Then there were the ten different items; sesame seeds, a cow, a piece of land, ghee, gold, silver, salt, cloth, grains, and sugar. These ten have to be given away as charity. When a man dies, all his sons have to take baths. The eldest son has to wear his sacred thread reversed as a sign of the inauspicious time. The dead body is washed and sacred ashes are smeared on it. Hymns invoking the Earth Goddess are sung.

Facing the page, on glossy paper, there was a photograph. The front veranda of a house in the style of houses in Mysore. The wall in the background had a window with an iron grill. On the floor of the veranda lay a corpse that had been prepared for the funeral.

The dead man is God. His body is Lord Vishnu himself. If it is that of a woman, then it is Goddess Lakshmi. You circumambulate it just as you would a god and you offer worship to it.

Then Agni, the sacred fire, is lit and in it ghee is poured as libation. The dead body gets connected to the fire with a single thread of cotton.

The big toes of the corpse are tied together and the body is then covered with a new white cloth.

There was a photograph of this also in the book. There was that same Mysore-style house. But in this photograph there were a few Brahmins with stripes of sacred ash on their foreheads and arms. The Brahmins even looked vaguely familiar. But then, from this distance, all ash-covered Brahmins of Mysore would look alike.

Four men carry the dead body on their shoulders. After tying the corpse to the bier, the corpse's face turned away from the house, the funeral procession starts.

The corpse is then taken to the cremation grounds for cremation. Once there, it is placed, head toward south, on a pile made out of firewood. The toes are untied. The white cloth covering the body is removed and is given away to the low-caste caretaker of the cremation grounds. The son and other relatives put grains of rice soaked in water into the mouth of the corpse and close the mouth with a gold coin. Excepting a piece of cloth or a banana leaf over the crotch, the corpse is now naked as a newborn baby.

'Where would they get a gold coin? These days who has got so much gold? Would fourteen-carat gold do?' Do the scriptures approve it? he wondered.

The eldest son then carries on his shoulder an earthern pitcher filled with water. A hole is made in the side of the pitcher. Carrying it on his shoulder, the son trickles the water around the corpse three times. Afterwards, he throws the pitcher over his back, breaking it.

There was a photograph of the cremation too. Looking at it, Annayya became a little uneasy because it looked somewhat familiar to him. The photograph was taken with a good camera. The pile of wood built for the cremation; the corpse; and a middle-aged man, the front of his head shaved in a crescent, on his shoulder a pitcher with water spouting from it; trees at a distance; and people.

Wait a minute! The face of the middle-aged man was known to him! It was the face of his cousin, Sundararaya. He had a photographic studio in Hunsur. How did this picture come to be here in this book? How did this man come to be here?

On the next page, it was a photograph of a blazing cremation fire. At the bottom of the photograph were printed the hymns addressed to Agni, the God of Fire.

O Agni! Do not consume this man's body. Do not burn this man's skin. Only consign him to the world of his ancestors. O Agni, you were born in the sacrificial fire built by this householder. Now, let him be born again through you.

Annayya stopped in the middle of the hymn and turned the pages back to look again at cousin Sundararaya's face. He had no spectacles on. Instead of his usual cropped grey hair fully covering the head, the front half of the head was tonsured into a crescent just for this ritual occasion. Even the hair on his chest had been shaved off. He wore a special Melukote dhoti below his bulging navel. But why was he here in this book?

Annayya turned to the foreword. It said that this Fergusson chap had been in Mysore during 1966–8 on a Ford Foundation fellowship. It also said that, in Mysore, Mr Sundararaya and his family had helped him a great deal in collecting material for the book. That is how the photographs of the Mysore houses came to be in this book. Once again, he flipped through the photographs.

The window with the iron grill—it was the window of his neighbour Gopi's house, and the one next to it was the vacant house that belonged to Champak-tree Gangamma. Those were houses on his own street. And that veranda was the veranda of his own house. The corpse could be his father's. The face was not clearly visible. It was a paralysed face, like a face he might see under running water. The body was covered in white. The Brahmins looked very familiar.

The author had acknowledged his gratitude to Sundararaya, his cousin: he had taken the author to the homes of his relatives for ritual occasions such as a wedding, a thread-wearing, a first pregnancy, and a funeral. He had helped him take photographs of the rituals, interview people, and tape-record the sacred hymn. He had arranged for Fergusson to be invited to their feasts. And so, the author, this outcaste foreigner, was very grateful to Sundararaya.

Now it was becoming clear. Annayya's father had died. Cousin Sundararaya had performed the funeral rites because the son was abroad, in a foreign land. Mother must have asked people not to inform him of his father's death. 'He is all alone in a distant land; the poor boy should not be troubled with the bad news. Let him come back after finishing his studies. We can tell him then. Bad news can wait.' Probably all this was done on the advice of this Sundaru, as always. If Sundaru had asked her to jump, Mother would have even jumped into a well. Three months after Annayya came to the states, two years ago, Mother had written to him that Father could not write any more letters because his arms had been paralysed. Who knows what those orthodox people have done now to his widowed mother! They might even have had her head shaven in the name of tradition. Widows of his caste cannot wear long hair. He became furious, thinking about Sundararaya. The scoundrel! The low-caste *Chandala*! He looked at the picture of the cremation again. The window with the iron grill. The corpse. Sundararaya's head shaved in a crescent. His navel. He read the captions under the pictures again.

He turned the pages backwards and forwards. In his agitation, the book fell flop on the library floor. The pages got folded. He picked up the book and nervously straightened the pages. The silence there until now had been broken by the roaring sound of a waterfall, a toilet being flushed in the American lavatory down the corridor. As the flushing subsided, everything was calm again.

He turned the pages. In the chapter on *seemantha*, the ceremony for a pregnant woman decked up like Princess Sita in the epic, wearing a crown on her head, his cousin's daughter. Damayanti sat awkwardly among many married matrons. It was her first pregnancy and the bulge around her waist showed that the pregnancy was quite advanced. Her father, Sundararaya, must have arranged the ceremony conveniently to coincide with the American's visit so that he could take photographs of the ceremony. He must have scouted around to show the American a cremation as well. And he got it, conveniently in his own uncle's house. 'How much did the Fergusson chap pay him?' wondered Annayya.

He looked for his mother's face among the women in the picture but didn't find it. Instead he found there others whom he knew: Champak-tree Gangamma and Embroidery Lachchamma. The faces were familiar, the bulb noses were familiar, the ear ornaments, the nose studs, the vermillion mark on the foreheads as wide as a penny, were all familiar.

Hurriedly he turned to the index page. Looked under V: Veddas, Vedas, Vestments. Then under W: Weber, Westermarck, West Coast ... at last he found widowhood. There was an entire chapter on widowhood. Naturally. In that chapter, facing page 233, was a fine photograph of a Hindu widow; her head clean-shaven according to the Shaivaite custom, explained the caption. Acknowledgements: Sundarrao studio, Hunsur. Could this be his own mother in the photograph? A very familiar face, but quite unrecognizable because of the shaven head and the edge of the saree drawn over her face. Though it was a black-and-white photograph, he knew at once the saree was red. A faded one. The kind of saree only widows wear.

Sundararaya survived that day only because he lived 10,000 miles away, across the whole Pacific Ocean, in a street behind the Cheluvamba Agrahara in Hunsur.

Translated by Narayan Hegde

GLOSSARY

chandala   A representative Sanskrit term for the untouchables, many of whom performed graveyard and cremation duties.

holeya   Also known as *pulayar* and *parayar*, the holeya community belongs to the dalit caste and is one of the main social groups found in Kerala, Karnataka, and Tamil Nadu.

nagaswara   Wind instrument used in south Indian classical music, often played during auspicious occasions such as weddings.

seemantha   ceremony performed during the eighth month of the first pregnancy in the husband's house.

vina   a string instrument, also used in south Indian classical music.

QUESTIONS FOR DISCUSSION

Reading the Story

1. Did you expect this story to take such a bizarre turn? What was your reaction?
2. The story raises many issues. Can you list them?
3. This story is steeped in irony. Discuss.
4. Ramanujan has used interpolations from other texts, breaking the straightforward narrative. The story is all the more convincing because of this. Explain.
5. Would you agree that the story is a comment on the anthropologist as voyeur?

6. 'You want self-knowledge? You should come to America.' Do you think this is a reflection on Annayya too?
7. At the end of the story, does Annayya's enthusiasm for scholarship give way to disenchantment?
8. Ramanujan takes a wry look at conservative Hinduism. Pick out passages that demonstrate this.
9. Do you think this story would work just as well in English?

Translation Issues

10. The task of an anthropologist is similar to that of a translator. Do you agree? If so, why?
11. Do you think the translator's task was made more difficult because the author had included quotes from ancient texts? Elaborate.

Activities

12. Do you know anyone who lives between two cultures? Do a brief character sketch based on your observations (200 words).
13. Ramanujan is a well-known translator, poet, and folklorist. Read any one of his works.
14. Study any one ritual practised by your community carefully. Write about it.

[handwritten notes]

So, several differences to the other texts I am reading in this essay

→ Kannada, not English

→ A story about the Indian migrants to the West

→ A look at India from outside (but also shapes/minds)
   — curious tension here

→ The insider has to go outside in order to gain a comprehensive understanding of India
   (or so he thinks — does the text show him up?)

MALAYALAM

MALAYALAM

LALITHAMBIKA ANTHERJANAM (1909–85)

Born in 1909 in a Namboodiri household in the state of Travancore, Lalithambika Antherjanam was taught Malayalam and Sanskrit at home and encouraged to read widely. However, as a Namboodiri woman, she was confined to the women's quarters as soon as she came of age. She was shaped as a writer by the reform movements and the nationalist movement taking place at the time. Most of her fiction first appeared in newspapers and magazines. She also wrote a series of essays based on women characters from the Ramayana and the Mahabharata. While she has written poetry, the short story was her preferred form. After her first collection, which came out in 1937, eleven more volumes appeared—among them *Kalathinde Edukal*, *Moodupadathil*, and *Koddumkattil Ninnu*. In 1976 she published her one and only novel, *Agnisakshi*, which won her the Vayalar award and the state as well as central Sahitya Akademi awards. Her memoir *Atmakathakkoru Amukkham* is also well known. A collection of her stories, *Cast Me Out If You Will*, translated by Gita Krishnakutty, was published in English.

മരത്തൊട്ടിൽ

വളരെ വളരെ നാൾക്കുമുമ്പ് - എന്നു വെച്ചാൽ മുപ്പതു വയസ്സായ ഒരു യുവതിയുടെ ഓർമ്മശക്തിക്കെത്താവുന്നതിലേറ്റവും അങ്ങേ അറ്റത്തുവെച്ചു നടന്ന സംഭ വങ്ങളാണവ - വെറും മൂന്നരയും ഒൻപതും വയസ്സിനിടയ്ക്കുള്ള ഒരു കുട്ടിക്ക്, അതും ബാലികയ്ക്ക്, പഴംകഥകൾ കേൾക്കുവാനുള്ള കൗതുകത്തെപ്പറ്റി നിങ്ങൾക്കൊക്കെ അറിയാമല്ലോ. അവൾ കാണുന്നതിന്റെയൊക്കെ കാരണത്തെപ്പറ്റി അതുമിതും ഇങ്ങനെ ചോദിച്ചുകൊണ്ടിരിക്കും. ഒരു വൃദ്ധയായ പരിചാരിക കൂടി സ്വാധീനത്തിലുണ്ടെങ്കിൽ പിന്നെ പറയാനുമില്ലല്ലോ. അടുക്കളപ്പൂച്ച സദാ 'മ്യാവൂ മ്യാവൂ' എന്നു വിളിക്കുന്നത് ആരെ യാണെന്ന് അവൾക്കറിയണം. ആ പൂച്ചയും തങ്ങളുടെ വളർത്തുനായും തമ്മിൽ എപ്പോഴും കടിപിടി കൂട്ടുന്നത് അവര് ചേട്ടാനിയന്മാരായതുകൊണ്ടാണോ? തോട്ടത്തിലെ കുരുവിക്കൂട്ടിൽ നിന്നു രാവിലെ തള്ളക്കിളി തീറ്റിതേടി പുറത്തുപോയാൽ കുഞ്ഞു ങ്ങൾക്കു പേടിയാവില്ലേ? നീലനിറമായ ആകാശത്തിൽ അങ്ങിങ്ങു പറന്നുനടക്കുന്ന വെള്ളമേഘപ്പക്ഷിയുടെ കൂട് എവിടെയാണ്? രാവിലെയും വൈകിട്ടും എന്നും ഇങ്ങനെ കുകുമച്ചെപ്പു തട്ടിമറിച്ചാൽ മാനത്തെ അമ്മ കുഞ്ഞുങ്ങളോടു കോപിക്കില്ലേ? ഇങ്ങനെ ഇങ്ങനെ പോവുന്നു ജിജ്ഞാസയുടെ ആ കുരുന്നു നാമ്പുകൾ....

ഒരു ധനികകുടുംബത്തിലെ ഓമനയ്ക്ക് പരിചാരകരോടെടുക്കാവുന്ന പല ദുസ്സ്വാതന്ത്ര്യങ്ങളുമുണ്ട്. ഒരു മനുഷ്യക്കുരുതിയുടെ കഴുത്തിൽ കയറിമാത്രമേ സവാരി പോവുകയുള്ളൂ എന്നു പതിവാക്കാം. ഒരു ഗ്ലാസ്സു പാലുകുടിക്കണമെങ്കിൽ പത്തു നുണ ക്കഥകൾ പറയണമെന്നു വാശിപിടിക്കാം. അവസാനമില്ലാത്ത വികൃതിപ്പണികൾ വിട്ട് ഒന്നുറങ്ങണമെങ്കിൽ വൃദ്ധദാസി അവൾക്കറിവുള്ളതും ഇല്ലാത്തതുമായ നാടൻപാട്ടുകൾ മുഴുവൻ പാടണം.

അമ്പിളിയമ്മാവൻ അന്തിയാവോളം അലഞ്ഞ് ഭാര്യയ്ക്കും കുട്ടികൾക്കും വിശ പ്പുമാറ്റുവാൻ ഒരുപിടി പൊടിയരിയുമായി ആകാശത്തിന്റെ ഒരറ്റത്തുനിന്നു മറ്റേ ചെരുവി ലേക്കു പോരുകയായിരുന്നു. വഴിക്കു കാലിടറി അരിമുഴുവൻ ചിതറിപ്പോയി. അതാണു നക്ഷത്രങ്ങൾ!

ബാലഹൃദയത്തിന്റെ കൗതുകം ഇടയ്ക്കു കയറി ചോദിക്കുന്നു. "ഇപ്പോഴും ആ കുഞ്ഞുങ്ങൾ വിശന്നു കരയുകയാണോ?...."

Wooden Cradles*

These are events that took place a long time ago, events that go as far back as the memory of a thirty-year-old woman can take her. You all know how much a little child between the ages of three and nine, especially a little girl, delights in listening to someone telling old legends. And if she has an old woman servant at her command, her happiness is complete. She asks a thousand questions, and must be given reasons for everything that happens. Whom does the kitchen cat call out to when it mews all the time? Why are the cat and the dog at each other's throats? Is it because they are brothers? When the mother sparrow goes out from the nest every morning in search of food, aren't the baby sparrows afraid to be by themselves? Doesn't the sky mother get furious when her children overturn her box of vermillion every day, morning and evening? And so they sprout, endlessly, the young tendrils of curiosity.

The cherished darling of a wealthy family can exercise many unjust privileges over the servants in the household. She will ride nothing but a human horse. She must be told a dozen stories before she will drink a glass of milk. At the end of a crowded day, if she must desist from further mischief and go to sleep, her old slave must sing every song she knows.

Uncle Moon was exhausted, for he had been wandering all day in search of food for his starving wife and children. At last, by dusk, he had found a handful of broken rice grains. On his way home across the vast sky, he slipped and the rice grains scattered and became stars!

The little one interrupts to ask innocently, 'And are the children still crying for food?'

When the sky turns dark, when lightning flashes, and the thunder roars, we know that the Lord of the Skies is preparing for war. The Great

---

*Marathottil

One, the Sun, set out in his royal chariot to marry the daughter of the Lord of the Skies. A demon stopped him on the way and would not let him go on. The Lord of the Skies whirled his sword. The thunder you hear is the demon roaring in pain. And the raindrops you see are the tears of the bride and her attendants, distraught with the fear that the wedding will never take place.

Infant logic must clear a doubt, 'And did the wedding take place?'

We all learned our first lessons in life from such women. It was forbidden to swim in the tank next door because two people once drowned in it; if little girls went to play under the *elanji* tree, a *yakshi* would tear them to pieces; if you played with your shadow, you would be born a demon in your next life. As we approach the last stage of childhood, these old women begin to seem as useless to us as antiquated wooden cradles. Their hands suddenly feel coarse and rough. And yet, the crude images that those roughened nails once etched on the tender walls of a child's mind continue to gleam fitfully beneath the veneer of time, now clear , now indistinct.

Once I was thirteen, I had no time for Nangelipennu. Her house was a good ten miles from ours. She had come to us when she was eleven years old, when my father was still a child. She had lived with us, a part of the family for sixty-two years, till she was old and helpless. No one in her family had cared to arrange a match for her, so she had never married. Although she was unmarried she always had children whom she could call her own. Their jewels were hers and their toys too. She shared their illnesses and all their pleasures. One by one, each child in the family became her charge. As she relinquished each little one who had learned to walk on its own, another newborn was placed in her arms. She would hold it close and proudly chant:

> God gave this little baby
> To parents who longed for one.
> God gave this little baby
> To Nangeli who longed for one.

She had sung generations of babies to sleep with her cradle songs, her affection flowing generously from father to daughter, uncle to nephew. Every child in the family grew up under her care. And yet, when she fell seriously ill in her seventy-third year with rheumatic pains and chills, our foster mother had no home that she could call her own.

When Nangelipennu left us, my youngest brother, the eighth in the family, was three years old. She bathed him, placed a *thilakam* on his forehead, dressed him in a silk shirt and trousers, and kissed him, her eyes full of tears. 'Who will be Nangelipennu's baby now?'

He was my mother's last child. There would be no more babies in the *tarawad*. Nangelipennu was old and sick now and she no longer wanted to stay in a house where the other servants jeered at her. She was far too proud to stay where she was not needed. All the same, she was unutterably sad when she said goodbye to us. She kissed each of us children in turn and then asked me, in a voice choked with tears, 'Will you think of me, child, when you're married and living happily with your husband? I'll come for your wedding'.

I was furious. I hated anyone talking to me about marriage. Two of my younger aunts had recently been married, and both had left the house weeping. They seldom came home now. Who would look after my flowerpots, my pictures, my cupboard, my books, if I went away as they had done?

'In that case,' I said gruffly to Nangelipennu, 'you need never come back.' And I moved away from her.

She often asked my eleven-year old brother, 'When you've got your BA, and all, what will you give Nangelipennu?' He detested her, would never go to her. 'Get away from me. You'll stain my clothes with your snot!' In the end, Nangelipennu realized what had happened—all the little ones whom she had hatched in the loving warmth of her hands had become birds that soared in the skies. They would find tall trees to build nests in, they would revel in the wide firmament. They would never come back to the little nest of broken twigs they had once been content with.

One of Nangelipennu's distant relatives had a granddaughter who had a baby every year. She couldn't go out to work because of the little ones. Nangeli *amma* arrived and took charge. Over the next four years, she had the good fortune to have five babies to care for. None of the children wanted their mother, they preferred their new grandmother.

The years went by. Despite all my protests, I had to give in and get married. Nangelipennu did not come to my wedding. Instead her granddaughter brought us the news, 'It started with a fever and a chill. She didn't even last two hours. Oh, Amme, the little one is still crying. She refuses to eat because she wants her grandmother.'

In time, I had a baby too. I hunted everywhere for a live wooden cradle that would keep my child away from fire and water, calm him when he cried, and look after him with care. The memory of Nangelipennu came alive again and touched my heart. The old servant had been dead for years now. No one like her could be found in our part of the country. Her granddaughter had her own children and grandchildren to look after. Indeed all the mothers and grandmothers I knew had children of their own to care for.

After a long and arduous search, I found someone named Bhanumathi. She was fourteen, had never handled babies before, and was herself a child. When the baby cried, she would not come anywhere near him. And, anyway, it would have been no use if she did, the baby burst into tears every time he saw her cross face.

I caught myself remembering the innumerable ways in which Nangelipennu used to coax a fractious child into good humour again. She would twist her lips in an expression of reproach, widen her eyes hold out her arms, and say, 'Did you hear the drums, little one? There he comes, the *kavadi* man.

With a young moon in his hair
He comes, on a blue peacock,
Velavan, my savior!
Haroharo!hara!

If you don't come with me, little one, Nangelipennu will go off by herself.' Which child could resist her invitation?

From our upstairs window, we could see the Nagamala range, enveloped in clouds. Two strange rock formations that looked like demons covered in smoke lay between two of its peaks. They were known as 'Pandi' and 'Pandiyathi'. Whenever a child cried, Nangelipennu would say, 'Look at Pandi and Pandiyathi. God turned them into rocks because they were obstinate and willful.'

The most disobedient child would give in to this threat, for no one wanted to turn into a rock that could not move. And then, of course, Nangelipennu had to repeat the oft-told story once more, with new embellishments. She would sit on the floor, her legs outstretched, eager to start, and the children would crowd around her, their eyes wide with delight saying, 'Tell us, how did Pandi and Pandiyathi turn into rocks?'

Drumming gently on her knees, the old storyteller would begin:

Once upon a time, in the kingdom of Pandi, there lived a king and a queen. The king had a gold chariot that took him wherever he wanted to go, and the queen had a gold chain that gave her whatever she wished for. One day they came to hunt in Nagamala.

The king, tired and thirsty after a long day's hunt, sat down on a rock. There was not a drop of water anywhere near. He prayed, 'Lord of Nagamala, if a pond appears here now, I'll make you a handsome offering.'

Amazing! A spring gurgled toward them from the top of the mountain. They took a handful of water in the hollow of their hands and drank, and their hunger and thirst were quenched.

The exhausted queen prayed, 'Lord of the Mountain! If you build me a palace here, I too will make you a worthy offering.'

Astonishing! A seven-storey mansion appeared magically. Its floor was of gold, its walls of precious gems. The king and the queen slept in it and woke up on the third day. They were loath to leave. The king said, 'If I sell the entire Pandi kingdom, I'll never have as much gold as there is here. Let's take as much as we can in our chariot.'

The queen said, 'I'll not find a single gem as lovely as these in the whole treasury. I must have one for my chain.'

Disgusted with their cupidity, God decided to punish them. 'You can stay here forever and enjoy the gold and the gems.' And he turned them both into rocks. So you see, my children, how evil greed can be.

These grandmother's tales, which have their origin in superstitions, stay long in our minds, complete with a moral that is related to life. But the women who narrated them, women like Nangelipennu are no more. Today's children no longer have old-fashioned wooden cradles, they have pretty bunched ones of fine net. Old sweet country songs have been forgotten and recorded music has taken their place. But the heart of a child does not change. One day when thunder roared and rain swished down, my son asked me, 'What is that thudding on the roof, Amma?'

I knew what it was: sea water becomes water vapour, rises, cools, and falls as rain. When clouds collide, sparks of electricity are ignited, and there is lightning and thunder. I knew, but all the same, I said to him, 'It is the Lord of the Skies making ready for war.'

Translated by Gita Krishnankutty

GLOSSARY

kavadi   A bent piece of wood that is beautifully decorated, carried on a devotee's shoulders, connoting sacrifice at every step. It is shaped like a wooden bow, decorated with peacock feathers and flowers, and is carried by pilgrims to the Subramania temple.

tarawad   an extended Namboodiri/Nair household

thilakam   mark drawn on the forehead

yakshi   A demigoddess or spirit

QUESTIONS FOR DISCUSSION

Reading the Story

1. This story was written in 1941, but it is relevant even today. Does it strike a chord in you? Elaborate.
2. Reflect on your own life and the society around you. Discuss the resonances that the story has for you.
3. How does Antherjanam convey the mind of a child?
4. Antherjanam has captured the unequal nature of the relationship between Nangelipennu and the children of the household. What does this say about our society?
5. The writer has seamlessly woven in stories within the story. Comment.
6. Written in the first person, the story seems to convey a strong sense of felt experience. Does this add to the success of the story?
7. The narrator is deeply introspective, almost reprimanding herself for not having valued Nangelipennu enough. How does this come through?
8. Is there an underlying tone of nostalgia in the story? Comment.

Translation Issues

9. It is difficult to translate songs. How effective has the translator been?
10. Would you consider it a challenge to translate folk tales and grandmother's tales?

Activities

11. Rewrite the story from the point of view of Nangelipennu.
12. Write a brief first-person account of childhood. You might want to talk about the caregivers who looked after you.
13. Write a grandmother's tale you have heard as a child.
14. Choose a story in an Indian language you are familiar with, which deals with a childhood completely different from your own. Translate into English a passage that made an impact on you.

Vaikom Muhammad Basheer (1908–94)

One of the greatest writers Malayalam has ever produced, there is no one quite like Basheer. Active in the freedom movement, Basheer had very little by way of formal education. Yet his active engagement with life by way of working at all kinds of professions from a loom fitter to a cook, and a fortune teller doubtless enriched his writing. His was a fresh voice that broke the bastions of traditional, Sanskritized Malayalam literature. Basheer came to writing quite accidentally. His first story was written when the editor of *Jayakesari* offered to pay him a small fee in return for a story. Most of Basheer's stories, outrageous and larger than life, are drawn from his rich and varied life. His wide canvas can include just about anyone: a prostitute, a card-sharper, a schoolteacher, and a holy man. His writings have cast a magical spell over generations of readers. His works in translation include *Katha Classics: Vaikom Muhammad Basheer* (edited by Vanajam Ravindran), *Poovan Banana and Other Stories* (translated by V. Abdulla), and *Me, Grandad, and an Elephant!* (translated by R.E. Asher).

Photograph: courtesy Punalur Rajan

വിശ്വവിഖ്യാതമായ മൂക്ക്

അമ്പരപ്പിക്കുന്ന മുട്ടൻ വാർത്തയാണ്. ഒരു മൂക്ക് ബുദ്ധിജീവികളുടെയും ദാർശനികരുടെയും ഇടയിൽ വലിയ തർക്കവിഷയമായി കലാശിച്ചിരിക്കുന്നു. വിശ്വവിഖ്യാതമായ മൂക്ക്.

ആ മൂക്കിന്റെ യഥാർത്ഥ ചരിത്രമാണ് ഇവിടെ രേഖപ്പെടുത്താൻ പോകുന്നത്.

ചരിത്രം ആരംഭിക്കുന്നത് അദ്ദേഹത്തിന് ഇരുപത്തിനാലുവയസ്സു തികഞ്ഞ കാലത്താണ്. അതുവരെ അദ്ദേഹത്തെ ആരും അറിഞ്ഞിരുന്നില്ല. ഈ ഇരുപത്തിനാലാ മത്തെ വയസ്സിനു വല്ല പ്രത്യേകതയുമുണ്ടോ എന്തോ. ഒന്നു ശരിയാണ്. ലോകചരിത്ര ത്തിന്റെ ഏടുകൾ മറിച്ചുനോക്കിയാൽ മിക്ക മഹാന്മാരുടെയും ഇരുപത്തിനാലാമത്തെ വയസ്സിനു ചില പ്രത്യേകതകൾ കാണാൻ കഴിയും. ചരിത്രവിദ്യാർത്ഥികളോട് ഇതെടുത്തു പറയേണ്ട കാര്യമില്ലല്ലോ?

നമ്മുടെ ചരിത്രപുരുഷൻ ഒരു കുശിനിപ്പണിക്കാരനായിരുന്നു. കുക്ക്. പറയത്തക്ക ബുദ്ധിവൈഭവമൊന്നുമുണ്ടായിരുന്നില്ല. എഴുത്തും വായനയും അറിഞ്ഞു കൂടാ. അടുക്കളയാണല്ലോ അദ്ദേഹത്തിന്റെ ലോകം. അതിനു വെളിയിലുള്ള കാര്യങ്ങ ളെക്കുറിച്ച് തികച്ചും അശ്രദ്ധൻ. എന്തിനു ശ്രദ്ധിക്കണം?

നല്ലവണ്ണം ഉണ്ണുക; സുഖമായൊന്നു പൊടിവെലിക്കുക; ഉറങ്ങുക;വീണ്ടും ഉണ രുക;കുശിനിപ്പണി തുടങ്ങുക. ഇത്രയുമാണ് അദ്ദേഹത്തിന്റെ ദിനചര്യ.

മാസങ്ങളുടെ പേർ അദ്ദേഹത്തിനറിഞ്ഞുകൂടാ. ശമ്പളം വാങ്ങേണ്ട സമയമാ കുമ്പോൾ അമ്മ വന്നു ശമ്പളം വാങ്ങിക്കൊണ്ടുപോകും. പൊടിവേണമെങ്കിൽ ആ തള്ള തന്നെ വാങ്ങിച്ചുകൊടുക്കും. ഇങ്ങനെ സുഖത്തിലും സംതൃപ്തിയിലും ജീവിച്ചുവരവേ അദ്ദേഹത്തിന് ഇരുപത്തിനാലു തിരുവയസ്സു തികയുന്നു. അതോടെ അത്ഭുതം സംഭവി ക്കുകയാണ്!

വേറെ വിശേഷമൊന്നുമില്ല. മൂക്കിനു ശകലം നീളം വെച്ചിരിക്കുന്നു. വായും കഴിഞ്ഞു താടിവരെ നീണ്ടുകിടക്കുകയാണ്!

അങ്ങനെ ആ മൂക്ക് ദിനംതോറും വളരാൻ തുടങ്ങി. ഒളിച്ചുവെക്കാൻ പറ്റുന്ന കാര്യമാണോ? ഒരു മാസംകൊണ്ട് അതു പൊക്കിൾവരെ നീണ്ടു. എന്നാൽ, വല്ല അസുഖവുമുണ്ടോ? അതുമില്ല ശ്വാസോച്ഛ്വാസം ചെയ്യാം.

The World Renowned Nose[*]

It is sensational news. A nose has become a topic of controversy among intellectuals and political thinkers. A world-renowned nose!

I record here the true story of that nose.

The owner of that world-renowned nose had completed twenty-four years of age when the story began. No one knew him before that. Does the twenty-fourth year in a person's life have any special significance? Who knows? If one looks through the recorded pages of world history one finds that the twenty-fourth year had a significance in many great lives. Students of history need hardly be told this.

The hero of our story was a cook, a kitchen worker if you like. He was not particularly intelligent. He could not read and write. His world was confined to the kitchen. He was totally indifferent to happenings outside it. Why should he pay attention to them? He could eat to his satisfaction; take as much snuff as he wanted, sleep, work. His daily routine was confined to these activities.

He did not know the names of the months of the year. When it was time for him to receive his salary his mother would come and collect it. If he wanted snuff the old woman herself would buy it for him. He lived a contented life till he reached his twenty-fourth year. Then an amazing thing happened!

His nose grew slightly in length. It passed his mouth and reached the level of his chin.

The nose began to grow in length every day. Was it possible to hide this? Within a month the nose reached his navel. Did he feel uncomfortable? Not in the least! He could breathe freely. There was no inconvenience worth talking about.

However because of his nose the poor cook was dismissed from his work.

---

*Viswavikhyatamaya Mookku

What was the reason?

No group came forward with the battle cry, 'Take back the dismissed employee.' Political parties shut their eyes to this piece of blatant injustice.

'Why was this man dismissed?' No lover of humanity came forward with this query.

The poor cook!

No one needed to tell him why he had lost his job. The reason was that the people living in the house where he worked could find no peace or quiet because of him. People came visiting night and day to see the Long-Nosed One. Photographers pestered the family. News reporters became a nuisance. A number of things were pilfered from the house.

As the dismissed cook sat starving in his lowly hut he was convinced of one thing—his nose had acquired great publicity!

People from distant lands came to see him. They stood stunned with surprise at his long nose. Some touched it too. But no one asked, 'Have you eaten today? Why do you look so weak?' There was no money in the hut, not even to buy a small packet of snuff. Was he a wild animal to be kept starving? He might be a fool, but he was a human being. One day he called his old mother aside and told her in a whisper, 'Get these horrid people out and shut the door!'

The mother promptly sent them all out and closed the door.

Good fortune came to the mother and son from that day. People began to bribe the mother to see the son's nose! Some upholders of justice protested against this corruption. But the Government did not take any action. Many protested against the inaction of the Government and joined revolutionary parties to sabotage the Government!

The income of the Long-Nosed One grew day by day. Need one say more? In six years the poor cook became a millionaire.

He acted in three films. What vast audiences were attracted by the Technicolor feature film, *The Human Submarine!* Six poets wrote epic poems about the noble qualities of the Long-Nosed One. Nine well-known writers wrote biographies of the Long-Nosed One and won wealth and acclaim.

His princely abode was also a guest-house open to all. Anyone at any time could get a meal there; and a bit of snuff.

He had two secretaries. Two comely, accomplished women. Both of them loved the Long-Nosed One. Both of them worshipped him. When two beautiful women love the same man at the same time there is bound to be trouble. Troubles came into the life of the Long-Nosed One.

Other people also loved the Long-Nosed One; that long nose reaching down to the navel was considered a sign of greatness. The Long-Nosed One gave his opinion on important world events. Newspapers published his comments:

'An aeroplane with a speed of 10,000 miles an hour has been built! The Long-Nosed One commented on the event—!'

'Doctor Bundrose Furasiburose has brought a dead man to life! The Long-Nosed One made the following speech about it—!'

When people heard that the highest peak in the world had been scaled, they asked, 'What does the Long-Nosed One say about this?'

If the Long-Nosed One said nothing about an event ... Poo! It was unimportant. The Long-Nosed One was expected to comment on anything and everything! Art, the watch trade, mesmerism, photography, the soul, publishing houses, the writing of novels, life after death, the conduct of newspapers, hunting.

It was at this time that conspiracies were hatched to capture the Long-Nosed One. To capture something, taking something by physical conquest, was nothing new. The major part of world history consists of conquests and captures.

What does it mean to capture? Suppose you plant coconut seedlings on a piece of barren land. You water the land and manure it. You fence it in. Expectant years slip by and the trees bear fruit. Coconuts hang in proud clusters from the palms. Then someone takes that garden away from you.

First of all, it was the Government that made an attempt to capture the Long-Nosed One. They tried a trick. The Government awarded him the title 'Chief of the Long-Nosed Ones' and gave him a medal. It was the President himself who tied the jewelled gold medal round the neck of the Long-Nosed One. Then, instead of shaking the Long-Nosed One by the hand, the President tweaked the tip of the long nose. This was filmed by newsreel cameramen and shown in all the theatres.

By that time the political parties in the country had come forward enthusiastically. Comrade Long-Nose must give leadership to the people's struggle! Comrade Long-Nose indeed! Whose Comrade? Comrade in what? Great God! Poor Long-Nosed One!

The Long-Nosed One must join The Party! Which party? There were many parties. How could the Long-Nosed One join so many different parties at the same time?

The Long-Nosed One said in his own tongue, 'Why should I join a party or parties? Me, I am too tired.'

Then one of the secretaries said, 'If Comrade Long-Nose likes me he must joint my party.'

The Long-Nosed One said nothing to that.

'Need I join any party?' the Long-Nosed One asked the other secretary. She guessed what he was aiming at. She replied, 'Why should you?'

By that time one of the political parties had come out with the slogan: 'Our party is the Long-Nosed One's party, the Long-Nosed One's party is the people's party!'

Members of other parties were incensed by this. They got at one of the secretaries and made her issue a scathing statement against the Long-Nosed One: 'The Long-Nosed One has deceived the people! He has been cheating them all this while. He has made me a partner in this fraud. Let me declare the truth to the public—the long nose is made of rubber!'

What a statement! All the newspapers splashed the news on their front pages. The nose of the Long-Nosed One is made of rubber! Would the people keep quiet at this? Would they not react in rage? Cables, telephone calls, and letters came from all parts of the world! The President was allowed no peace or quiet. 'Destruction to the rubber nose of the Long-Nosed One! Down with the Long-Nose Party! Long live revolution!'

When the anti-Long-Nose Party put out this statement, the opposing party made the other secretary issue a counter-statement: 'Beloved countrymen, citizens! What she has said is a lie. Comrade Long-Nose did not love her and this is her revenge. She was trying to keep for herself the wealth and good name of Comrade Long-Nose. One of her brothers is in the opposite party. Let me reveal the true colours of the members of the other party. I am the faithful secretary of Comrade Long-Nose. I know for a fact that the nose of the comrade is not made of rubber. It is as real as my own heart beating inside me. Long live the members of the party supporting Comrade Long-Nose at this critical time! They have no motives of gain other than the progress of the people. Long live revolution!'

What was to be done? There was confusion in the minds of the people. The leaders of the party against the Long-Nosed One began finding fault with the President and the Government. 'Stupid Government! They gave the title "Chief of the Long-Nosed Ones" to a deceiver of the people. They gave him a jewelled gold medal. The President is also involved in this fraud. They have betrayed the national interest. The President must resign. The Ministry must resign! The Rubber-Nosed One must be killed!'

The President reacted angrily. One morning the army and their tanks surrounded the house of the poor Long-Nosed One. He was arrested and taken away.

There was no news of the Long-Nosed One for some time. The people forgot about his existence. Then came fresh news with the impact of a nuclear bomb! Do you know what happened? Just when the people had forgotten everything came a brief announcement from the President: 'The trial of the "Chief of the Long-Nosed Ones" will take place on 9 March. Expert doctors who come as representatives of forty-eight countries will examine him. All the newspapers of the world will be represented by their respective correspondents. The proceedings will be filmed for all the world to see. The people must keep calm.'

People are people. They could not keep calm. They came in large numbers into the metropolis. They invaded the hotels. They burnt public conveyances. They set fire to police stations. They destroyed government buildings. There were communal riots. Quite a number of men and women died as martyrs in this fight for the Long-Nosed One.

9 March, 11 a.m. The square in front of the Presidential Palace was a vast sea of humanity. The loud speakers blared forth: 'People must be disciplined. The examination has begun!'

The doctors surrounded the Long-Nosed One in the presence of the President and cabinet ministers. One doctor blocked the nostrils of the Long-Nosed One; he immediately opened his mouth wide. Another doctor took a needle and punctured the tip of his nose. To his amazement a drop of blood appeared at the tip of the nose.

The doctors gave their unanimous verdict: 'The nose is not made of rubber. It is genuine.'

One of the female secretaries kissed the Long-Nosed One on the tip of the nose.

'Long live Comrade Long-Nose! Long live the "Chief of the Long-Nosed Ones"! Long live the Progressive People's Party of the Long-Nosed One!' As this shouting and revelry ended, the President thought of another gimmick. He nominated the Long-Nosed One as a Member of Parliament! 'The Honourable Long-Nose M.P.!' Three universities conferred doctorates on him. 'The Honourable Long Nose-D. Litt!' The ignorant populace acclaimed the actions of the equally ignorant Government which ruled over them.

But the parties of which the Long-Nosed One was not a member formed a United Front and began to proclaim: 'The Ministry must resign! This is a fraud on the people! It's a rubber nose!'

Look at the way falsehood was being perpetuated! Would there not be confusion of thought? What could the poor intellectual do?

Translated by V. Abdullah

GLOSSARY

darshan   a viewing, usually of a deity or a holy person

QUESTIONS FOR DISCUSSION

Reading the Story

1. How does Basheer use humour in this story to comment on society?

2. Does this story remind you of others that you may have read? Discuss Basheer's writing.

3. Basheer uses an absurd situation to poke fun at various people. Who are they?

4. What does Basheer really think of politicians and their ideology? Even intellectuals and the media are not spared. Comment.

5. In what way does Basheer comment on the mentality of ordinary people?

6. Discuss the underlying serious tone of the story. Did it prompt you to reflect on life in an altogether different way?

7. The intimate tone of the story and the narrative style suggest that Basheer is sharing a joke with readers. Cite examples from the text.

Translation Issues

8. Humour is often difficult to translate. How has the translator dealt with Basheer's humour?
9. Basheer is known for his colloquialisms. Pick out instances where the translator has dealt with them successfully.

Activities

10. Basheer has a wide range of stories, many of them available in English translation. Read one that is completely different from 'The World Renowned Nose'.
11. Write a funny piece using an absurd situation.
12. Rewrite the story from the nose's point of view.

PAUL ZACHARIA (b. 1945)

Paul Zacharia is one of Kerala's best-known writers. His stories move through a wide range of moods from the gently mocking and teasingly funny to the reflective and even violent. Highly unorthodox, Zacharia's unsentimental prose flies in the face of established literary conventions. To him even the ordinary moments in life sizzle with possibilities. He is a recipient of the Sahitya Akademi Award and the Katha Award. Zacharia is known for his experiments in narrative techniques and believes it is important for writers to react to social issues. His works in translation include *Bhaskara Pattelar and Other Stories* (translated by Gita Krishnankutty, A.J. Thomas, and the author), *The Reflections of a hen in Her Last Hour and Other Stories* (translated by A.J. Thomas and the author), and *Praise the Lord and What's New, Pilate? Two Novellas* by Paul Zacharia (translated from the Malayalam by Gita Krishnankutty).

ലാസ്റ്റ് ഷോ

കാമുകൻ തന്നെയുപേക്ഷിച്ചു എന്നു വിശ്വസിക്കുന്ന കാമുകി വിഷം തിന്നു ന്നു. വാസ്തവത്തിൽ തനിക്കു രക്താർബുദമാകയാലാണ് കാമുകൻ കാമുകിയുമായി അകൽച്ച നടിക്കുന്നതും തന്റെ സ്നേഹം മറച്ചു വയ്ക്കുന്നതും. കാമുകൻ ദരിദ്രനായ ഒരു ഗായകനായിരുന്നു. ധനികയായ കാമുകിയാണ് അയാളെ ജീവിതവിജയത്തിലെ ത്തിക്കുന്നത്. നിരാശയിൽ മുഴുകിയ കാമുകി അച്ഛന്റെ ഉപദേശത്തിനു വഴങ്ങി മറ്റൊരു വിവാഹത്തിനു സമ്മതിക്കുന്നു വാസ്തവത്തിൽ ആ പ്രതിശ്രുതവരൻ കാമുകന് രക്താർബുദമാണെന്നു കണ്ടുപിടിച്ച ഡോക്ടർതന്നെയാണ് - മധുരയിലാണ് അയാൾ. കാമുകനും കാമുകിയും മദിരാശിക്കാരും. കാമുകൻ ഒരു കച്ചേരിക്ക് മധുരയ്ക്കു പോയ പ്പോഴാണ് രോഗം കണ്ടുപിടിക്കപ്പെടുന്നത്. നിശ്ചയതാംബൂലത്തിനു പ്രതിശ്രുതവരൻ മദിരാശിയിൽ എത്തുന്നു. അയാൾ കാമുകനെ ആകസ്മികമായി കാണാനിടവരിക മാത്ര മല്ല, അയാളെ വാസ്തവമറിയാതെ, കാമുകിക്കും, അച്ഛനും പരിചയപ്പെടുത്തിക്കൊടു ക്കുകയും ചെയ്യുന്നു. എന്തു രസകരമാണ് ആ രംഗം! ഞാൻ വായിലിട്ട പൊട്ടുകടല ചവയ്ക്കാതെ ആ സമാഗമം ആസ്വദിച്ചിരുന്നു. ഏതായാലും അവസാനം പ്രതിശ്രുതവ രൻ മുഖേന കാമുകി കാമുകനെപ്പറ്റിയുള്ള സത്യം മനസ്സിലാക്കുന്നു. പക്ഷേ, അപ്പോ ഴേക്കും അവൾ വിഷം തിന്നുകഴിഞ്ഞു. പ്രതിശ്രുതവരനും പിന്നാലെ മരണക്കിടക്ക യിൽനിന്നു കാമുകനും കാമുകിയുടെ അടച്ച വാതിൽക്കൽ പാഞ്ഞെത്തുന്നു. കാമുകി ഇഞ്ചിഞ്ചായി ഇഴഞ്ഞു വാതിൽ തുറക്കുകയും കാമുകനെ ഒരു നോക്കുനോക്കി മരിച്ചു വീഴുകയും ചെയ്യുന്നു. തുറന്ന വാതിലിലൂടെ കാമുകിയുടെ സമീപത്തായി കാമുകനും മരിച്ചു വീഴുന്നു. പക്ഷേ, അതിനുമുമ്പ്, കാമുകനെ കാണുന്ന കാമുകിയുടെ മുഖം ഒരു നിമിഷത്തേക്കു പാതി തുറന്ന വാതിലിലൂടെ ഒരു പുഞ്ചിരിയിൽ പ്രകാശമാനമാവു ന്നുണ്ട്. ആ പുഞ്ചിരി എനിക്ക് ഒരു കോരിത്തരിപ്പു നൽകി. ഒരു നിമിഷത്തേക്ക് ഒരു ശുഭാപ്തിവിശ്വാസം നൽകി. എല്ലാം ഇനിയും നന്നാകാൻ വഴിയുണ്ട്. പ്രതിശ്രുതവരനും നല്ലവനുമായ ഡോക്ടർ ഇരുവരെയും ഇനിയും രക്ഷപ്പെടുത്തും. കാമുകനും കാമു കിയും അയാളോടു നന്ദി പറഞ്ഞ് അവരുടെ ജീവിതങ്ങളുടെ പുതിയതും സന്തോഷം നിറഞ്ഞതുമായ ഒരധ്യായം തുറക്കും എന്നു ഞാൻ ആ പുഞ്ചിരിയുടെ ബലത്തിൽ പിടി ച്ചുതൂങ്ങി ആശിച്ചു. പക്ഷേ, വെറുതെ ഇരുവരും ഇലകൾ പൊഴിയും പോലെ സ്ലോമോ ഷനിൽ മരിച്ചു മറിഞ്ഞു വീഴുകയും പ്രതിശ്രുതവരനും മറ്റും അതു നോക്കി ഒരു ഫ്രീസ് ഷോട്ടിനുള്ളിൽ സ്തംഭിച്ചുനിൽക്കുകയും ചെയ്യുന്നു. മരിച്ചു വീണവരും ഒരു ഫ്രീസ് ഷോട്ടിനുള്ളിലാണ്, പിന്നെ വെള്ളിത്തിരമാത്രം. അതിൽ പ്രൊജക്ടറിന്റെ അവസാനത്തെ രശ്മികളിലൂടെ കാഴ്ചക്കാരുടെ തലകൾ ഉണ്ടാക്കിയ ഇളകുന്ന നിഴലുകൾ.

ഞാൻ തിയേറ്ററിന്റെ ആളൊഴിഞ്ഞ ഇടനാഴികളിലൂടെ നടന്നുചെന്നു.

The Last Show*

The heroine takes poison because she thinks that her lover has abandoned her. Actually, the hero only pretends to distance himself from her, and conceals his love for her because he discovers that he has blood cancer. He had been a poverty-stricken singer and it is the rich heroine who had helped him achieve success.

Plunged into despair by the hero's neglect, the heroine yields to her father's persuasion to marry someone else. Her fiancé is, in fact, the doctor who diagnosed her lover's cancer but she does not know this. He lives in Madurai. The hero and heroine live in Madras. The disease was diagnosed when the hero went to Madurai for a concert. The heroine's fiancé arrives in Madras for the *nischiathartham* ceremony. He meets the hero by chance and introduces the heroine and her father to him, unaware of all that has happened between his patient and his fiancée.

What an amusing situation! I even forgot to chew the *pottu kadala* in my mouth as I relished this encounter. Anyway, the heroine finally learns the truth about her lover from her fiancé. And she takes poison. Her fiancé rushes towards the closed door of her room on hearing the news, as also her lover from his deathbed. The heroine crawls painfully to the door, opens it, looks at her lover for a moment, and falls dead. Her lover collapses, falls into the room through the open door, and dies by her side.

Just before this takes place, however, a smile lights up the heroine's face as she catches sight of the hero through the half-open door. The smile made my flesh tingle. It led me to believe, for a moment, that all would be well, that there was still a possibility that things would end happily. It seemed to me that the heroine's fiancé, who was a doctor, and a man of excellent character as well, would be able to save both of

---

*Last Show

them. The hero and heroine would then express their gratitude to him and enter a new and joyful chapter of their lives. This is what I hoped would flow from the power of her smile. But what actually happens is that both of them slide down in slow motion, like falling leaves, and die, while the fiancé and others look on and are trapped in a freeze shot. The two dead lovers are also caught in a freeze shot. Afterwards, there is only the silver screen and the shadows of the viewers' heads as they get up and move through the last rays of the light from the projector.

I walked along the deserted corridor of the cinema house and climbed the steps to the projection room. I opened the door a little. The projectionist was rewinding the reels.

I said to him, 'So many possibilities were open to the hero and heroine, so many opportunities to change the course of their lives.'

He placed a reel in a round tin case.

I said to him, 'Shall we start the film tomorrow from the point at which the heroine smiles, and work out the possibilities it offers? Or else, we could hold back a reel or two and make some other changes. For example, if the hero does not go to Madurai for the music concert. ... Look, let us open these boxes and see what we can do. Do you have a pair of scissors?'

I leaned against the smooth body of the projector and pointed out many alternatives to him, many new directions that the hero's and heroine's lives could have taken. 'The heroine's dying smile, the smile that filled her face with such radiance, distresses me. I feel that a whole new life could have taken shape from it. Why didn't it happen that way? Can't you help me at all?'

He said to me, 'This was the last show, my friend. These boxes must leave town tomorrow.'

He put the last reel-case into a big box and closed it. Then he flashed a torch through the peep-hole in front of the projector and looked into the cinema house. I peered over his shoulder for a glimpse of the silver screen. But the light from the torch flickered and slipped into the darkness halfway down the length of the hall.

He flicked a switch and opened another little window. Lights came alive like stars in a night sky and began to glow all over the ceiling. We watched the lights for a while. Then he said, 'If only there was a moon as well!' I said, 'We need clouds too.' 'That's right,' he said, and wind and streaks of lightning. And also the possibility of sunrise 'and sunset.' He closed the peep-holes. 'And birds flying back to their nests at dusk.' I said.

As I went stumbling down the steps in the dark, I looked into the distant sky and saw the signs of a moonrise spread over the horizon, like the glow from an unseen pit of fire.

Translated by Gita Krishnankutty

GLOSSARY

nischiathartham   engagement ceremony
pottu kadala   fried gram

QUESTIONS FOR DISCUSSION

Reading the Story

1. Zacharia's narrative style is unusual. What did you think of this story? In what way is it different from the other stories in this collection?

2. How effective is Zacharia's comment on regional cinema?

3. Study the beginning of the story. It is a story within the story. Why has Zacharia employed this particular device?

4. This story has no linear narrative, no beginning or end, and no obvious morals. Yet it is powerful in its own way. Comment.

5. Zacharia comments on our fascination for formulaic films. Despite ourselves, we are irresistibly drawn towards them. Do you identify with the protagonist?

6. Notice the clever use of tense in the story. Would it have been just as effective if he had used the past tense to talk about the film story?

7. Film is a powerful medium. The heroine's smile seems to hold a happy possibility for the narrator. Do you think the written word is just as powerful?

8. What did you think of the bizarre conversation between the projectionist and the narrator?

9. This story is also visually very powerful. Did it work for you?

10. Would you read this story as a metaphor for life? The narrator comments on the many possibilities and endings on screen. Can this be applied to life as well?

11. Do you think the protagonist is vicariously living life through films?

Translation Issues

12. In the original, the translator had decided not to italicize terms such as 'nischiathartham' so as not to draw attention. Would it have worked for you? Discuss.
13. Would the story have been difficult to translate given its experimental style? Note the shift in tenses. How has the translator negotiated these tricky situations?

Activities

14. The film talks about the power of popular cinema. Write a story based on a popular film you have seen in any of the Indian languages.
15. Pick out a story without a linear narrative from any of the Indian languages. Translate the most challenging passage into English.

TAMIL

TĀMIE

C.S. LAKSHMI 'AMBAI' (b. 1944)

C.S. Lakshmi, scholar and critic, writes Tamil fiction under the name—Ambai. Highly innovative and experimental, her writing encompasses a wide variety of themes and styles. She deftly juxtaposes the old with the new, cleverly using myths and allusions, often linking them all with a fine thread of humour. No one story is like another. But above all, her concern for issues pertaining to women has invited much debate and discussion.

C.S. Lakshmi's critical work, *The Face behind the Mask,* is an analysis of the representations of women in modern Tamil fiction by women writers. She has established SPARROW, a Sound and Picture Archives for Research on Women.

Many of her stories have been translated by Lakshmi Holmström and have appeared as two collections: *A Purple Sea: Short Stories by Ambai* and *In a Forest, A Deer.* Katha has published *Ambai: Two Novellas and a Story.*

அணில்

ஆங்கில அரசாங்கம் புழங்கிய பழங்கால, அகன்று கிடக்கும் கட்டடங்களின் நீள் தாழ்வாரங்கள். முனை கூம்பிய வலை ஜன்னல்கள் அணைத்த தாழ்வாரங்கள். மேலே தோரணவாயில் சுவர் ஒவ்வொரு பத்தடிக்கும். வெய்யில் உள்ளே வராத மங்கிய தாழ்வாரங்களின் தோரணங்களின் கீழ் நடந்துகொண்டே போனால் அதன் இருள் முடிவில் இருப்பது புத்தகசாலை என்ற எதிர்பார்ப்பு. எதனால் என்று தெரியவில்லை. தாழ்வாரத்தில் கால் வைத்ததுமே அந்த எதிர்பார்ப்பு. வேகமுச்சு. வாயில் ஒரு எச்சில் ஊறல். நிறையத் தடவைகள் முனையில் புத்தகசாலைதான் நிஜமாகவே. பழுப்பாய் கிடப்பது. இரும்பு அலமாரிகளில் விழுந்து கிடப்பது.

ஒருமுறை. சீக்கிர இரவுகள் அப்போது. அஸ்தமனம் அப்போது தான் ஆகி முடிந்திருந்தது. தாழ்வாரத்தில் கால் வைத்ததுமே ஒரு முகம் அந்தரத்தில் மிதந்து வந்தார்போல் எதிரே. ஆந்தைக் கண்களிலிருந்தே கிளம்பி கன்னத்துச் சதை, கழுத்து எல்லாம் அருவி வழிவதுபோல், திக்கென்றது. ஜில்லிட்டுப் போயிற்று. சுருங்கித் தொங்கும் சருமத்தைத் தள்ளிவிட்டுச் சில பற்கள் தோன்றின புன்னகையில்.

"பயந்திட்டியாம்மா."

விளக்கு போடப்பட்டது. ஒரு நீண்ட தாழ்வாரம் உருப்பெற்றது. ஒரே தோரணச் சுவர்கள். குகைக்குள் போவதுபோல் உணர்வு. தாழ்வார முடிவில் சதுரக் கம்பிகள் போட்ட இரும்புக் கதவின் பின் மென்சிவப்பு ஒளி அடித்தது. இரும்புக் கதவின் மேலும் கீழும் ஒரு செம்புகை கவிந்திருந்தது. வேறு உலகத்துக்குத் திறக்கும் ஒரு நிழற் கதவாய் அது தெரிந்தது. அதைத் திறந்ததும் அங்கே சலங்கை ஒலியுடன் ஊர்வசி நடனம் இருக்கும் என்ற பிரமை தோன்றியது.

தாழ்வாரங்கள் இல்லாமல் சிறு சந்துகளில் போனாலும், எனக்கு அவை தாழ்வாரங்களாகிவிட்டன. எந்த நடைக்குப் பின்னாலும் பழுப்பாய், நாக்குகளைத் தொங்கவிட்டு மல்லாந்திருக்கும் புத்தகங்கள்தாம் என்ற எண்ணம். தொட்டு எடுத்தால் அட்டையில் ஒரு நாய்க்காது மடங்கல். அதை ஒட்டி ஒரு கீறல். அழுத்தமாக. வலிக்க வலிக்க. சில சமயம் புத்தகத்தின் முழு பாரத்தையும் தாங்காது முதுகு ஒடிந்திருக்கும். அங்கு தொட்டதும் 'தப்'பென்று ஓசை வரும். தடவி உயிர்ப்பித்ததெல்லாம் அகலிகைதான். எந்தக் காவியத்தில் இடம் பெறுமோ தெரியவில்லை.

Squirrel*

Long verandahs of spacious buildings which were once the offices of the British government. The verandahs are enclosed by meshed windows with angled tops. At every ten feet, there are ornamental arches above. As one walks along, passing under the arches of that shadowy verandah where the sun does not enter, one experiences a sense of anticipation, that at the end of the darkness there will be a library. Impossible to say why exactly, but one feels that expectation the moment one sets foot within the verandah. A quickening of the breath. A watering of the mouth. And often enough, it is there at the end, a library in truth. Yellowed. Stretched out in iron shelves.

One occasion. It was the time of year when it darkens early. The sun had only just set. As soon as I set foot on the verandah, there was a face as if suspended in space, floating in front of me. It was as if, starting from a pair of owl-like eyes, the flesh of the cheeks and neck had all slithered down like a waterfall. I was startled. I went cold. Then a few teeth appeared in a smile which pushed aside the wrinkled folds of skin.

'Were you frightened, madam?'

The light was switched on. A long verandah took shape. Endless archways. A sensation of entering a cave. At the end of it, a soft red light shone behind a steel door, chequered all over with steel wires. Above and below the door, a reddish smoke spread. It seemed like a shadowy door leading to a different world. I imagined that the instant the door opened, I would see Urvashi dancing to the sound of her own anklet bells.

(Whatever narrow passage I entered, to me it became a verandah. I began to think that at the end of every path, there were only old books, lying on their backs, their tongues hanging out. If you picked one up,

*Anil

you'd find a dog-eared fold on the cover. Next to that a scratch. Heavy. Painful. Sometimes the spine of the book was broken by its own weight. If you touched it there, you heard a sudden snap. Each book that was stroked and awakened to life was a very Ahalya. But which epic was there that recorded its history?)

The phantom door stood in front of me as material reality. He opened it. There was a small garden path. At the end of that a heavy wooden door stood open.

'They've all gone. I waited for you to come. Here is the book you asked for.'

There was a sudden gust of wind. The pages rustled, beating against each other. When I put my hand on the cover, pressing it down, the trembling of the leaves passed into me. The old man was no longer beside me. Except for the light in the front part of the building, all the others had been turned off. Open iron shelving reached up to the high ceilings. Inside, there were two upper levels, with iron-sheeted floors, reached by an iron staircase. I was alone, my hand resting on the book. In the corner, by the door, the rustling of the pages set off by the wind now joined into a thud-thudding sound. It was then that it appeared before me. It sat upon a pile of books which had just been mended with paste. It threw me a brief glance and began to lick the paste with great enjoyment.

'Don't do that,' I said. 'That's *Chintamani*, the women's journal that Balammal ran. That faded picture at the back, that's she in a nine -yard sari.'

(My relationship with her has only just begun. We have not yet conversed with each other. I don't as yet know everything about her, only that she was not all that fond of Vai.Mu.Ko.)

The squirrel listened. It took a quick look at Balammal and went away. The wind, the rustling of the pages, and the throbbing under my fingers continued.

All this had happened so often, both in dream and in reality, that I could no longer separate one from the other. Neither did it seem all that important to do so. It was a fact that the pages crumbled and fell to pieces beneath my fingers. A fact that the crumbling bits stuck to my fingers. A fact that the apsaras who first advertised Kesavardini hair oil crumbled away with those pieces. But this happened many times, both in dreams and reality. That's why I didn't try to separate the two. When

I was sure I was dreaming, the electric fan would suddenly stop and I would find myself bathed in sweat. Certain that it was real, I would raise a book in order to smell it, and be awakened by the raindrops splashing on to my face through the open window. I didn't worry about it. Isn't it possible that some relationships should extend from dreams into reality, and others be the spillover from reality to dreams?

A heavy dictionary, yellowing with age, lay upon a sloping desk by the window. When the wind blew, its huge pages would move. If I bent down, the pages touched my face. Moving, as if to stroke me, the pages would roll from 'B' to 'J'. And then the wind would stop. I would put it back to 'B'. One page alone would reach up to touch me affectionately on the cheek and then return to its place, leaving behind a faint smell.

I always move from one end of the open shelves to the other, touching the books. Establishing a relationship, I touch the dust as if I were caressing a naked child. I share a relationship with all of you, did you know? It was my fingers that smoothed the crease running through the centre of the letter which Mary Carpenter wrote in the nineteenth century, asking to set up a women's teacher training college. It was I who blew off the rust-coloured dust which had spread over the 'Rani Victoria Kummi' published in *Viveka Chintamani*. When a speck of that dust flew up against my lip, I flicked out my tongue and swallowed it. And so an older generation descended into my stomach. Perhaps if some Yasoda had looked into my mouth, she would have seen a Victoria Kummi.

It seemed that as soon as this library was set up, Krishna appeared in his chariot and preached his sermon of non-attachment there, giving as example the way water rolls off the lotus leaf. Nothing that the library contained touched anyone who was working here. Their only interest was in each one's knee-high stainless steel tiffin carrier. On the third floor, the Buckingham Carnatic Mill workers went on strike in May 1921. But downstairs the concerns were different.

'Ei, have you brought meat today? It smells good.'

'Yes, di. I cooked minced meat this morning. We don't eat meat for the whole of the month of *Purattasi*, and I have been feeling quite weak. My husband himself ground all the spices for me. But it's not yet time to eat. It's only twelve yet. Let's sit under the trees today. We'll take the water pot with us.'

'We could buy some betel leaf.'

'Watch out, Sir is coming.'

'Well, girls? Chatting about food are you? My wife says I must eat only fruit. She says I've got a paunch. I should have been lucky enough to be born a woman, to bear a couple of children, and then to bloat out and wear a chokingly tight *choli*.'

'Sir, it's true you've actually got a bit of a paunch. Maybe that's why she says that.'

'I shall have to be born a woman in my next birth. Then my flesh can hang around my waist, like Elizabeth's.'

'Why this, Sir? Why do you drag me into all this? There is no malice in me, sir. That's why I'm not as thin as a stick.'

'Are you going out to buy betel leaf? Get me half a dozen fruits.'

'Jackfruit, do you mean, sir?'

'Who said that? People come to work in this place half dead with hunger. Doesn't like my paunch, she says. Why can't she show me even a spoonful of ghee? What's lost if some onion tossed in butter is spread on a bit of bread for me? Don't I toil hard enough through the day? Now , you lot …'

'What have we done, sir?'

'Get on with your work, girls. Five lakhs of books are waiting to be catalogued. That's enough about minced meat and husbands who grind spices.'

Laughter.

Kk … kwik.

It came and sat upon the Factory Act. Once again it screeched .

'Look here, you are an eater of nuts. What business do you have here? Aren't there enough trees outside? What's there for you in this paste? Go and climb a tree. Go up. Come down. What sort of bad habit is this?'

All of a sudden it spread out its four legs on the book and lay prone on its stomach. A ray of sunlight, refracted through a hole in the window mesh, struck it softly on the head. It closed its eyes.

I did not touch it. I have no faith in miracles. Even if I did, I would not put it to the test. I am not used to conversing with fairy princes.

The third floor was a somewhat neglected place. The man who catalogued Telugu books in one corner was given to muttering to himself every now and then. All the rest of the books were either torn, or just about to come apart, or had been pasted together in an effort to postpone death, and were waiting to be catalogued. The floor was of iron sheeting with a pattern of holes. Through these, you could see through to the ground floor. On one occasion, the book of chants used several years ago at the Madurai Meenakshi temple to exorcise evil spirits had slipped from my hands and fallen all the way down and on to the librarian's head.

And he had once climbed the ceiling-high open iron shelves in order to fulfil my wish, even forgetting his paunch.

'I can't reach to the top, sir, please look and tell me what there is up there.'

When he reached up there, he struck at the topmost stack of books with his hand. The dust rose in waves. When I craned my neck to look at him as he stood there, his legs spread apart and planted firmly on the shelves facing each other, his head immersed in clouds of dust, one hand pressed against his chest to prevent an imminent sneeze, he seemed like the good, obedient genie who appears and demands work at the merest rub of the magical lamp.

'What's up there, sir?'

'Dust ... dust ... '

'No sir, what books?'

'I'll look, madam. There are lots of good books written, though, with my having to climb up like this for them. This is all rubbish, madam, rubbish.'

'If you want, I'll climb up, sir.'

'No, no, madam. This is my duty.' He sneezed about ten times. 'These are all just women's books, madam. Do you want them?'

'Throw them down, sir.'

They fell with a thud. First, *Penmadhi Budhini*, then *Jagan Mohini*. Several others followed. The notion of falling became closely linked in my mind with these books. It became an everyday occurrence to me to imagine them tearing their way through the roof and splitting their sides. For one who did not believe in miracles, I continued to experience a number of such illusions. When I touched the spine of an old mended nineteenth century book, an ecstatic tremor rose from the soles of my feet and passed through me. When Anna Sattianadhan lay upon her deathbed, asking her husband to pray for her, there were only I and the squirrel on the third floor to share her grief. The evangelist who rode horseback to propagate Christianity broke through the meshed windows of this same third floor. When a Bengali girl set fire to herself after leaving a note for her father, telling him he must not sell his only house in order to meet her marriage expenses, the flames chased through this very place like snakes. The flames spread throughout the third floor and disappeared, having revealed their form only to the squirrel and me. The Telugu catalogue was not there that day.

What the third floor contained was not just books, but a whole generation, throbbing with life. Respectable older women in nine yard saris, with shoes upon their feet and rackets in hand, played badminton with white women. Many preached untiringly to young women, how best they could please their husbands. They took great pains to explain the dharma that women should follow, addressing their readers as my 'girl', and putting on compassionate faces. Nallathangal chased her son even when he pleaded with her to let him go, pushed him into a well, and jumped in after him. When a Brahmin stubbornly refused to do the last rites upon a girl who was an unshaven widow, her knee-length hair was removed from her very corpse. *Devadasi*s dedicated to temples sang, 'I cannot bear the arrows of *Kama*,' as they danced to the point of exhaustion. Gandhi addressed women spinning at their charkas, Uma Rani of *Tyaghabhumi* rang out, 'I am no slave.' In the women's pages, 'Kasini' wrote about new styles in bangles. The cover-girl of *Ananda Vikatan* swept along, swinging her arms while her husband carried her shopping bag. Taamaraikanni Ammal proclaimed, 'We will sacrifice our lives for Tamil.' Her real name—a Sanskrit one—was Jalajakshi. Ramamrutham Ammal confronted Rajaji head on when he wrote that Gandhi would not come unless he was paid money.

All, all these women were present there. And so was I. Sometimes they were weightless, as if made of smoke; at other times full of mass, heavy. The day the widow's head was shaved, a heaviness pressed upon my heart. Razor-blades appeared everywhere. Each lock of hair fell away with a loud sound. Each lock of hair rubbed abrasively against my cheek. I came to life only when the squirrel tapped its tail twice and raised the dust. It was leaning against the issue of *Kalki* which had Ammu Swaminathan on the cover. Apprently it had finished eating up the paste.

I looked downward through the holes in the floor. The librarian's head was eased back against the chair. On the desk, a file inscribed,

Subject: STRING. This was his favourite file. Three years ago it had been a shining violet in colour, now it was fading and dog-eared. The file began with a letter requesting some string so that the old magazines could be sorted out and tied according to their months and years. Back came the answer that it was not customary to supply string to libraries and demanding a full explanation for breaking this rule. Following upon this were other letters. If the magazines were not separated according to their months, they became chaotic and useless. Useless to whom? To researchers. Which researchers? Were they from Tamil Nadu or elsewhere? And so it went on. One day the librarian pulled out a ball of string from his trouser pocket. After this he wrote a letter asking to be reimbursed for the cost of a ball of string, which set off another series of letters. Every day the file would appear on his table. The money had still not been paid.

The squirrel screeched. *Keech keech*. My only link with reality. At the same time my companion in the world of illusions.

Yes, I know. It is late. The paste is finished. But I haven't the mind to leave these women. There seems to be a magical string that links us. I hear them speak. As Shanmuga Vadivu strikes the first note of the octave upon her *vina*, the sound floods into my ears. K. B. Sundarambal sings, 'Seeking the bright lotus, seeing it, the bee sings its sweet song … utterly lost.' And Vasavambal, accompanying her on the harmonium joins in with 'utterly lost.' On the Marina beach, Vai. Mu. Ko. hoists the flag of Independence. The women who oppose the imposition of Hindi go to prison, their babes in their arms.

Look, this is another world. That paste should have made you aware of at least a taste of it. A world which we share, you and I.

'Are you coming down, madam?' He was smiling as he looked up and called out.

'In a minute.'

He came up.

'We've been sent the Rule.'

'What Rule?'

'It's very expensive to mend and repair all this. Not many people read them either. Perhaps one or two like you. How can the government afford to spend money on the staff and paste and so on? They are going to burn the lot.'

'Burn what?'

'Why, all these old unwanted books?'

Not a single thought rose in me. Except for one, at the edges of my mind. So the file on string has finally been closed. Only its burial is left now.

'Come, madam.'

I came to the iron stairs and then turned to look. The evening sun and the mercury lamp combined to spread an extraordinary light on the yellowing books, like the first flood of fire that spreads over a funeral pyre. Then he put out the light.

Darkness mingled with the dim red light, turning it into deep crimson, like magical flames. The squirrel lay prostrate in front of the window, its four legs spread out, in an attitude of surrender.

As I climbed down the stairs, a small wave of thought hit me: that window faces north.

Translated by Lakshmi Holmström

GLOSSARY

Ahalya	Wife of Rishi Gautama. She was seduced by Indra who deceived her into believing that he was her husband. The Rishi cursed her, turning her into a stone. In Pudumai Pittan's (1906–48) retelling of the legend in his story, *'Saba Vimochanam'*, Ahalya, on learning that Rama required Sita to undergo a trial by fire, chooses to turn into a stone again, rather than live in Ayodhya.
apsara	Celestial nymph/dancer.
Buckingham Carnatic Mill ... strike:	When a British officer entered the mill with a revolver, one of the workers snatched the gun and ran away. A case of an attempt to murder was registered against the worker, and the mill was subsequently closed. The workers went on a hunger strike and were fired upon, resulting in the death of a woman worker. The Factory Act, mentioned later in the text, was formulated after this strike.

Chintamani	A journal founded in 1924 by Sister Balammal for improving the condition of women and for disseminating knowledge among them. A representative issue included articles on heroic Indian women, stories from the epics, and pieces of popular interest such as Marco Polo's travels.
choli	a tight-fitting blouse worn with a saree.
di/da	Term of familiarity used between equals or to address those younger than oneself.
Jagan Mohini	A women's magazine.
Kama	Hindu God of love.
Mary Carpenter	(1807–77). British philanthropist and social reformer who supported the movement for higher education for women. She established a National Indian Association to inform English opinion on the needs of India.
North	The reference is to vadakkirutal, a ritual described in the earliest Tamil poetry: in protest or sorrow, one fasted to death facing northwards.
Penmadhi Bodhini	First women's magazine in Tamil, started in 1891.
Rani Victoria Kummi	Kummi is a group dance performed by women on auspicious occasions. The dancers move in a circular pattern, clapping their hands rhythmically, and singing songs. 'Rani Victoria Kummi' was a Kummi in praise of Queen Victoria.
Tyaghabhumi	Title of a film scripted by Kalki and also serialized in the 1930s. Uma Rani is the chief character.
Urvashi	A heavenly nymph in Hindu mythology, renowned for her beauty and her skill in dancing.
Vai.Mu.Ko.	Vai.Mu.Kodainayaki Ammal (1901–60): A Gandhian and one of the first Tamil women

to wear and to advocate the use of khadi. She was also the editor of a journal and a popular novelist who published more than 115 novels. She was married at the age of five and had no formal schooling. Her novels dealt with widow remarriage, the uplift of devadasis, and other social issues.

vina   musical instrument used in classical Indian music.

Viveka Chintamani   A journal founded in 1892 and edited by C.V. Swaminatha Iyer.

QUESTIONS FOR DISCUSSION

Reading the Story

1. Did you find the story unusual and thought-provoking? Why?
2. Do a 'close reading' of the text. Read and re-read the story as many times as you like so that you grasp all the nuances and connotations. Notice the vocabulary, the style, the imagery, the theme, etc. What view of the world do you think the author offers?
3. What did you think of Ambai's description of the library? Discuss the narrator's relationship with the books.
4. The story slides effortlessly between dream and reality. What effect did this have on you?
5. A word about the last line of the story which refers to *vadakkirutal*. (See glossary for 'north'). Notice how cleverly and effortlessly Ambai juxtaposes the old with the contemporary, making associations with bygone traditions. What bearing does this have on the ruling to burn the old journals?
6. Why do you think Ambai has used the whimsical, playful squirrel which lends a light touch to such a richly textured story?
7. The story has an unusual protagonist: a woman interested in women's history is sifting through old journals. There is a strange and different sense of adventure in what she is doing: '*What had appeared on the third floor were not mere books; they were whole generations throbbing with life*'. Did Ambai recreate the past for you? Did the period, the characters, and their lives come alive?

Translation Issues

8. This story carries quite a few explanations in the glossary. Would the story have worked for you without them? Why do you think the translator has used them?

9. A translator's job is not merely to translate a story. Oftentimes, she has to interpolate in order to place things in proper perspective for a reader not familiar with the literary tradition of the original. Pick out an example from the text where you think the translator has elaborated to make the meaning clearer. Discuss.

Activities

10. If you have competency in any of the Indian languages, pick up an issue of a popular magazine or journal that was published at the time of the nationalist struggle. Notice the concerns of the time, the style of writing, the layout, the kind of products advertised, etc. Do they seem old-fashioned to you?

11. Down the ages, the relationship of women to culture has been different from that of men. Their literary works have often been dismissed as trivial and uninteresting, very limited in scope. Many of our older women writers have creatively expressed themselves against tremendous odds. Think of the lives of the older women in your own family and their struggles as women. How did they express themselves creatively? In anonymous ways such as embroidery and cooking, or did they leave behind a diary/journal? Reflect on your own life. Has it been shaped by the efforts of the women of the older generation?

12. Visit the archives closest to you (if this is not possible, visit a good college library) and describe your experience in a paragraph. Make it as vivid and descriptive as possible, taking special note of details.

13. Write about the importance of the space of a library in your own life. Do you have enough time and space for your private reading? Very often, other distractions intrude into the space we have set apart for reading and reflecting. The library then seems to be our only refuge. Do you agree?

14. Read a story by a contemporary woman writer in an Indian language you know and render at least a page into English (if you know Tamil, translate a paragraph of Ambai's 'Anil' into English).

Read a story now by a woman from an older generation and translate at least a paragraph into English. Compare the two experiences. Notice that no two translations will read the same.

ASHOKAMITRAN (b. 1931)

Ashokamitran is one of the best-known and most widely translated of Tamil writers. Having lived in Secunderabad and Madras, it is the urban landscape with its commonplace occurrences that deeply interests him. His wry, ironic gaze doesn't miss a detail, and he can turn the most ordinary of events into an epiphanic moment. His novels and short stories are marked by subtle satire and an engrossing portrayal of people who thrive despite hardships. His works include *The Colours of Evil* (translated by N. Kalyan Raman), *My Father's Friend* (translated by Lakshmi Holmström), *A Most Truthful Picture and Other Stories* (translated by the author et al.), *Sand and Other Stories* (translated by N. Kalyan Raman and Gomathi Narayan), *The Eighteenth Parallel* (translated by Gomathi Narayan), and *Water* (translated by Lakshmi Holmström).

எலி

இரண்டாவது நாளாக இப்படிச் செய்ததில் கணேசனுக்கு மிகவும் கோபம் வந்தது; இன்றைக்கும் இரவுச் சாப்பாட்டிற்குப் பிறகு ஒன்றையும் மீதம் வைக்காமல் சமையலிடத்தை ஒழித்துப் போட்டு அவன் போட்டு அவன் வீட்டுப் பெண்மணிகள் படுத்து விட்டார்கள். அப்படி ஒன்றும் விவரம் தெரியாதவர்களில்லை. அக்காவுக்கு ஐம்பது வயதாகிறது. மனைவிக்கு நாற்பது முடியப் போகிறது. மகளுக்குப் பதின்மூன்று வயது வரப்போகிறது. ஒரு தோசைத்துண்டு, ஒரு அப்பளத்துண்டு, ஒரு தேங்காய்ச் சில்லு கிடையாது. எலிப் பொறிக்கு எதை வைக்கிறது? எக்கேடு கெட்டுப் போங்கள் என்று கணேசனும் படுத்து விட்டான்.

அரைமணி தூங்கியிருக்கமாட்டான், துணி உலர்த்தும் மூங்கில் கோல் அசைவது கேட்டது. எலி கோலடியில் சுற்றிக்கொண்டிருக்கிறது. இரு நிமிஷங்கள். இப்போது கோல் இன்னும் அதிகமாக அசைகிறது. எலி கோல்மீது ஏறிக்கொண்டிருக்கிறது. இப்போது பித்தளைத் தாம்பாளம் சுவரில் இடிக்கும் சப்தம் கேட்கிறது. எலி பரண் மீது ஏறிவிட்டது. கசகசவென்று சப்தம். எலி பழைய செய்தித்தாள் குவியல் வழியாக முன்னேறிக்கொண்டிருக்கிறது. தடக்கென்று ஒரு சப்தம். எலி பரணிலிருந்து மரப் பீரோவுக்கு தாவி விட்டது. பீரோ மீது போட்டிருந்த காலித் தகர டின்கள் கடகடவென்கின்றன. எலி பீரோமீதிலிருந்து சுவரில் ஆணி அடித்து மாட்டப்பட்டிருக்கும் அலமாரிக்கும் போய்விட்டது. சிறிது நேரம் எல்லாம் அமைதியாக இருக்கிறது. அதற்கு ஈடு செய்வது போல் தடாலென்று ஏதோ கீழே தள்ளப்படுவது பெரிதாகக் கேட்கிறது. இப்போது கணேசன், அவன் மனைவி இருவரும் எழுந்து விளக்கைப் போட்டுப் பார்க்கிறார்கள். எலி எண்ணெய் ஜாடியின் மூடியைக் கீழே தள்ளிவிட்டிருக்கிறது.

மனைவி அரைத் தூக்கக் கண்ணுடன் எண்ணெய் ஜாடியை மூடி அதன்மீது ஒரு கூடையைக் கவிழ்த்து வைக்க அவளைப் பல்லைக் கடித்தவண்ணம் கணேசன் பார்த்து நின்றான். ''ஏதாவது மிச்சம் வைச்சுத் தொலைலன்னா ஏன் இப்படித் தினம் துடைச்சு துடைச்சு வைக்கிறே?'' என்று கேட்டான்.

''என்னத்தை மிச்சம் வைக்கிறது? ரசத்தை எலிக்கு வைக்கறதா? இல்லெ, உப்புமாவை பொறிக் கொக்கியிலே மாட்டி வைக்கறேளா?'' என்று அவள் கேட்டாள்.

''நீ என்னன்னு நினைச்சுண்டிருக்கே?'' என்று கணேசன் கேட்டான்.

The Rat*

That they had done it for two nights in a row made Ganesan very angry. Not sparing a single morsel, the ladies of his household had polished the kitchen clean after the night's meal and gone off to bed.

It wasn't as though they didn't know any better. Sister was over fifty. Wife was pushing forty, and Daughter was soon going to be thirteen. But not a scrap of *dosai*, or *appalaam*, not a sliver of coconut was left over.

What was he supposed to use as bait for the rat-trap?

'To hell with the lot of you!' muttered Ganesan, and went to bed himself.

He had hardly slept a half hour when he heard the bamboo clothesline gently shaking. The rat was moving along its underside.

...Two minutes pass by. The bamboo line rattles a bit more. The rat is climbing on top of it. Now a brass tray can be heard banging against the wall. The rat has climbed into the loft. A crinkling, rustling sound. ... The rat is advancing steadily through a pile of old newspapers. Dhadak! The rat jumps down from the loft upon the wooden bureau, setting off a clanking and clattering among the empty tins stored on top of it. The rat springs from the bureau to the small wall shelf hanging on a nail. Everything is quiet for a while. As though in compensation, something is knocked over and comes tumbling down with a big crash. ... Both Ganesan and his wife get up. The light is switched on, and they look around. The rat has knocked down the lid of the oil jar. ...

With clenched teeth, Ganesan stood glaring at his wife, who was sleepily putting the lid back on the jar and covering it with an upturned

---

*Eli

basket. 'When I tell you just keep some wretched thing or other left over, why do you daily polish off every bit like this?'

'Keep what? Should I keep a spoonful of *rasam* for the rat? Or maybe you can stick a lump of *uppuma* on the hook?' she asked.

'Just what do you think of yourself?' demanded Ganesan, incensed.

'Me? I'm not thinking anything. If there are dosais or adais, something can be saved for the rat. Daily in our house we are making dosais and *adai*s, isn't it?'

'Okay then, let the rat come daily! Let it spill and spoil everything!'

His wife did not reply. Instead, she fished out a dried-up onion from the bottom of the vegetable basket and gave it to him. 'Try this if you want.'

'When has any rat turned up to eat an onion like this?'

That onion he hurled at her must have caused her some pain. But she said nothing, and went back to bed.

Ganesan could not lie down. Every night in those two rooms, in that little space where the ten of them could not sleep or eat at the same time, four or five rats cavorted and frisked about with the utmost freedom. They gnawed and ripped through the clothes, pulled off the lids and toppled the tins, burrowed into tomatoes and devoured the insides, drank up the cooking oil. ...They dragged away the wick of the oil lamp in the gods' niche every single day, without fail.

He tossed on his shirt and put a quarter rupee into his pocket. Locking the front door behind him, he set out.

The regular hotels had all closed. Only tea stalls and betel shops were still open. If only he could find a *vadai*. Even half a vadai.

But nowhere were there any vadais left over. Bread, biscuits, bananas—only these remained, and they had all been tried out at one time or another. The rat had turned up its nose at all of them. Only oily things worked—deep-fried vadais, *pakoda*s, *pappadam*s. And at the price at which dal and oil were sold these days, how could such delicacies be made in the house? Rice uppumaa, *rava* uppumaa, *pongal*. Then pongal, rava uppumaa, rice uppumaa. After that rava uppuma, pongal, rice uppumaa. One after another after another, again and again—that was all that was to be had in that house. Ganesan was fed up with the very words 'uppumaa' and 'pongal'. That rat must have been fed up too.

Well, that rat's in luck, it must have peered into a fox's face first thing this morning, thought Ganesan. He turned homewards.

In the distant maidan, a public meeting was in progress. There were not more than thirty or forty people present. Yet somebody was flinging his arms about and giving a speech. Why not listen for a while? Ganesan walked towards the crowd.

The speaker was issuing a stern warning to Nixon. Another stern warning to China ... then to Britain, and to Russia. One to Pakistan. Then came a dire ultimatum to Indira Gandhi. Yet another to the leaders of Tamil Nadu. ... If a hundredth part of these terrifying threats could only reach the rat class, the whole pack of them would flee and seek asylum in the Bay of Bengal. Why didn't rats understand the Tamil language?

But something else was more to Ganesan's purpose than such talk. A little away from the crowd, several people were standing around a pushcart on which a stove had been fixed. With a long perforated ladle, sizzling hot snacks were being taken out of bubbling peanut oil and placed on a tray from which they were being sold off in bare seconds.

Ganesan went and stood near the pushcart. Like submarines immersed in the ocean, twenty chillies doused in batter were frying in the oil. A man nearby kept saying, 'Make vadais, *ayya*! Vadais!'. But the next time round it was chilli bajjis again. Ganesan, too, said, 'Make vadais, ayya!' There seemed to be a great demand for chilli bajjis. One fellow got out of a car, ordered, 'Pack up eight bajjis', and went to urinate into the darkness.

'Make vadais this time, 'ya', said Ganesan again. The moment the chillies were taken out of the oil, they were wrapped in pieces of newspaper and parcelled off immediately in twos, fours, even tens.

'Did you ask for vadais, saar? How many do you want?'

Ganesan felt hesitant to say he wanted just one. 'Two is enough,' he said.

'Then I'll fry them next time around.' Again it was chillies that were lowered into the oil. The man who had been demanding vadais for quite sometime began to protest belligerently.

'Here, this lot is almost done saar. Only one more minute! See, that gentleman over there is also waiting for vadais!'

An uneasy feeling came over Ganesan. There was a sizable crowd around the cart. Everybody was waiting for their orders. Waiting to eat.

…They must be thinking he too was waiting just as eagerly to eat his vadais. If they only knew that the vadai was for a rat-trap! He felt very unhappy.

When they were fried and ready at last, it was to him that two vadais were first given, on a piece of *Maalai Murasu*, the eveninger. The hot oil soaked through the paper and smeared his palm. They smelt very good, those two vadais. There were fragments of ground white dal sticking out of their tops.

Ganesan walked homewards. Unable to bear the heat, he had to keep tossing the vadais from one hand to the other. Hands and paper were all greasy. That pushcart vendor—poor fellow!—couldn't have known his vadais were destined to be eaten by a rat. Ganesan wouldn't have felt as bad about it if the vadais had been made in his own house. Now he felt quite troubled.

Impossible, without ruining his shirt, to take the key out of his pocket with his oily hands. He put the vadais down and wiped the oil on his shins and the loose, slack flesh of his calves. Going into the house he stuck one vadai on the hook of the rat-trap. The other one he ate. …

When a man over fifty eats a vadai at ten o' clock in the night, there are bound to be consequences. But he made himself think of them as a kind of expiation. He lay down, and at last slept off.

Morning. Ganesan's stomach was in utter chaos. The rat had got caught in the trap and made a terrible racket all through the night. He himself knew nothing about it; it was his wife who told him.

Now the rat had to be taken somewhere and let loose. He picked up the trap and set out. The rat poked its nose out of a little hole in the trap. From that nose it couldn't be made out if it were a big rat, or a small one. However, if it could knock down a tin of flour, topple the lid off the oil jar, chew up soiled clothes, and gnaw at vegetables, what difference did it make whether it was big or small?

Not the gutter this time, thought Ganesan, and bore it off to the maidan. It would take at least a week for this particular rat to find the house again. Not that its absence mattered much. There were other rats.

… Can't these boys move off a bit, thought Ganesan. But they were waiting for him to open the rat-trap. He put it down on the ground and gently pressed the handle of the lid. The rat ran out. It was neither very big nor very small. Unaccustomed to wide open spaces it rushed around confusedly in all directions. One of the boys threw a stone.

'No, boy!' cried Ganesan.

Just then a crow came flying out of nowhere, pecked once at it and flapped off. The rat lay twitching on its back, then scrambled up and dragged itself along even faster. Above, the crow circled once, and then swooped swiftly down. The rat had nowhere to hide itself. The crow now snapped it up and carried it away. Ganesan felt a pang.

Something else made him even sadder. When he picked up the trap and turned to go home, he took a look inside. The vadai he had stuck on the hook the night before still hung there, uneaten.

Translated by Vasantha Surya

Translator's Note

The eatables referred to in this story are common south Indian main dishes and 'tiffins' or snacks based on rice and dal. Apart from the well-known dosai, there is the adai, a thicker lentil pancake, and the appalaam, which is a lentil crisp. Rasam is a clear lentil soup. Uppumaa is a broken wheat savoury, pongal is a sweet or savoury mash of rice and dal. Vadais, pakodas, and pappadams are all deep-fried snack foods.

GLOSSARY

maidan   open ground

QUESTIONS FOR DISCUSSION

Reading the Story

1. Notice the urban setting of this story, so different from that of 'The Chair'. How does the author bring alive city life?
2. This story could have happened to any one of us. How has the author woven such a wonderful story from such a commonplace event?
3. The author has an eye for detail. Which descriptions appealed the most to you? Discuss.
4. Even such an ordinary task as buying vadais is a funny adventure in itself. In our mind's eye, we can clearly see Ganesan in the maidan, listening to the dramatic speech, buying vadais, etc. Discuss how the author successfully employs humour to carry the story through.

5. What did you think of the way the story ends? Discuss the ironic, tragic elements. Would you agree that Ganesan is, in a funny way, attached to the rat?
6. Why does the sight of the uneaten vadai make Ganesan sad?
7. How does the author indicate that Ganesan and his family do not have much money? Does it have a bearing on the story?
8. As readers, we get a sense of the cramped urban space in which the story takes place. Contrast it with the village setting in 'The Chair'.

Translation Issues

9. The conversations in the story are fresh and immediate. The translator has used English as it is spoken in Tamil Nadu today, heavily influenced by Tamil lexis and syntax. Would it have been as vibrant and colourful if the translator had used standard English?
10. The translator has provided a note at the end of the text about common south Indian snacks. Would it have been as effective had she not used Tamil terms such as vadai, uppumaa, etc.?

Activities

11. Have you thought of the importance of space in your life? How does it affect relationships? Write a paragraph drawing on your own experiences.
12. Ganesan's obsession with the rat may seem trivial, even amusing and bizarre. Recollect a commonplace incident in your life and make a funny story out of it.
13. The conversation between Ganesan and his wife, so amusing, is so true to life. Translate the conversation into any Indian language you are familiar with.
14. Translations of Ashokamitran's work are widely available. Choose any one story of his and compare it with this.

KI. RAJANARAYANAN (b. 1923)

Rayangala Shri Krishna Raja Narayana Perumal Ramanujam Naicker, or Ki. Ra, is both a storyteller as well as one of the most accomplished contemporary short story writers in Tamil. Even though he began writing only after the age of forty, he has won a number of awards, including the Sahitya Akademi award for his novel *Gopallapurathu Makkal* in 1991. Ki.Ra has been a visiting professor at the Pondicherry University, holding the post of Director of the Folktales, Documentation and Survey Centre. His focus is mainly on rural Tamil Nadu and his narrative skills owe much to oral traditions.

நாற்காலி

நாற்காலி இல்லாததும் ஒரு வீடா?

எங்கள் வீட்டில் இப்படித் திடீரென்று எல்லோர்க்கும் தோன்றி விட்டது. அவ்வளவுதான்; குடும்ப 'அஜெண்டா'வில் வைக்கப்பட்டு இந்த விஷயத்தில் விவாதம் தொடங்கியது.

முதல் நாள் எங்க வீட்டுக்கு ஒரு குடும்ப நண்பர் விஜயம் செய்தார். அவர் ஒரு சப்ஜட்ஜ். வந்தவர் நம்மைப்போல் வேட்டி சட்டை போட்டுக் கொண்டு வரப்படாதோ, சூட்டும் பூட்டுமாக வந்து சேர்ந்தார். எங்கள் வீட்டில் முக்காலிதான் உண்டு. அதன் உயரமே முக்கால் அடிதான், எங்கள் பாட்டி தயிர் கடையும்போது அதிலேதான் உட்கார்ந்து கொள்வாள். அவளுக்குப் பாரியான உடம்பு. எங்கள் தாத்தா தச்சனிடம் சொல்லி அதைக் கொஞ்சம் அகலமாகவே செய்யச் சொல்லியிருந்தார்.

சப்ஜட்ஜுக்கும் கொஞ்சம் பாரியான உடம்புதான். வேறு ஆசனங்கள் எங்கள் வீட்டில் இல்லாததால் அதைத்தான் அவருக்குக் கொண்டு வந்து போட்டோம். அவர் அதன் விளிம்பில் ஒரு கையை ஊன்றிக்கொண்டு உட்காரப்போனார். இந்த முக்காலியில் ஒரு சனியன் என்னவென்றால் அதன் கால்களுக்கு நேராகயில்லாமல் பக்கத்தில் பாரம் அழுங்கினால் வாரித் தட்டிவிடும். நாங்கள் எத்தனையோ தரம் உறியில் வைத்திருக்கும் நெய்யைத் திருட்டுத்தனமாக எடுத்துத் தின்பதற்கு முக்காலி போட்டு ஏறும்போது அஜாக்கிரதையினால் பலதரம் கீழே விழுந்திருக்கிறோம். பாவம் இந்த சப்ஜட்ஜும் இப்போது கீழே விழப் போகிறாரே என்று நினைத்து அவரை எச்சரிக்கை செய்ய நாங்கள் வாயை திறப்பதற்கும் அவர் தொபுகடீர் என்று கீழே விழுந்து உருளுவதற்கும் சரியாக இருந்தது. நான், என் தம்பி, கடைக்குட்டித் தங்கை அந்த சப்ஜட்ஜ் மாதிரியே கையை ஊன்றிக் கீழே உருண்டு விழுந்து காண்பிப்பாள், பின்னும் கொஞ்சம் எங்கள் சிரிப்பு நீளும்.

எங்கள் சிரிப்புக்கெல்லாம் இன்னொரு முக்கிய காரணம் அவர் கீழே விழும்போது பார்த்ததும் எங்கள் பெற்றோர்கள், தாங்கள் விருந்தாளிக்கு முன்னால் சிரித்து விடக்கூடாதே என்று வந்த சிரிப்பை அடக்கிக் கொண்டதை நினைத்துத்தான்!

ஆக நாங்கள் எல்லார்க்கும் சேர்த்துச் சிரித்துவிட்டு வீட்டுக்குள் பூனைபோல் அடி எடுத்து வைத்து நுழைந்து பார்த்தபோது அந்தப் பாரியான உடம்புள்ள விருந்தாளியைக் காணவில்லை. அந்த முக்காலியையும் காணவில்லை.

The Chair*

A house without a chair?

Everyone in our house suddenly began to feel this way. And that was it: the matter was placed on the family 'agenda', and the debate commenced.

A friend of the family had paid us a visit the day before. He was a sub-judge. The man could have come in a veshti and shirt like any of us, couldn't he? But no, he had to turn up in 'suit-boot'. All we had in our house was a three-legged stool whose total height was just three-fourths of a foot. *Paati*, our grandmother, always sat on it when she churned the curds to make butter. As her figure was on the plump side, our grandfather had got the carpenter to make the seat a little extra broad.

The sub-judge, too, was a little on the portly side. There being nothing else in the house for him to sit on, we brought out the stool. He leaned one hand on its edge and attempted to seat himself. One fiendish thing about this three-legged stool was that if you leaned on one side of it instead of depositing your weight directly on top, it would fling you down. We had fallen from it so many times whenever we failed to observe this precaution before climbing on it to steal a taste from the ghee-jar hanging from the rafters. Just as we were thinking, 'Poor sub-judge! He's going to fall!' and were about to open our mouths to warn him, he had toppled and was rolling on the floor.

Unable to hold back our laughter, the three of us—my younger brother, our youngest sister who was the baby of the family, and I—raced to the back garden. Whenever the howls were about to subside, my sister would do an imitation of the sub-judge leaning his hand on the stool and keeling over. This would prolong our laughter. A further cause for mirth was the memory of how our parents had struggled to remain polite and suppress their own laughter as their guest took a tumble.

---

*Naarkaali

When the three of us had finished giggling and tiptoed back into the house like pussy cats, there was no sign of the portly sub-judge. Or of the three-legged stool. 'Has he taken it with him?' asked my baby sister innocently.

It was after this event that the decision was taken to get a chair made for the house. But there was a practical difficulty: no sample was available. There wasn't a single chair in our village. Neither was there a carpenter who knew how to make one.

'So let's buy a ready-made chair in town and bring it here, that's all,' was our big brother *Peddanna*'s idea. My father rejected it, saying no city chair would prove durable. Then *Athai*, our paternal aunt, came forward with the information that a highly competent carpenter was available in a nearby village. To hear Athai tell it, not only was there no style of chair he didn't know how to make, but the Governor himself had bestowed high praise on the chairs he made.

When she heard the second part of Athai's little speech, Mother's look said, Yes, yes! She's seen everything! She pointedly turned her face away.

Appa called the servant and sent him to the village to search out that far-famed carpenter. Discussions began on the kind of wood to be used for making the chair.

'Teak, of course,' said Paati. 'Only a chair made of teak will be easy to lift and to put down, and yet be strong and sturdy.' She sat with her legs stretched out in front of her, stroking her calves and shins. Our paati was very fond of her legs.

At this moment, in walked *Maamanaar*, our maternal uncle.

Peddanna ran inside and brought out the three-legged stool. For a while the very house shook with laughter before things settled down.

Actually, however, Maamanaar was in no danger. He always sat in the same spot whenever he came to our house. Chop off his head, and he'd still sit there and nowhere else. It was the southern corner of the front hall. Having seated himself on the floor, leaning against the pillar which stood there, the first thing he always did was to unwind his tuft and shake out his long hair. Then he would give his head a good scratching and tie up his tuft again. This was his unvarying habit. Having done this, he would peer closely at the floor around him. Peddanna would pretend to join the search. With an impudent smile he'd remark, 'It doesn't look as though you've dropped any coins around here!'

Whenever Maamanaar came to our house, we tried to riddle him with our jokes and pranks. They fell like paper arrows on him. It's only my son-in-law's family making fun of me, after all, he seemed to say serenely, without actually opening his lips—like a stone *Pillaiyaar* by the wayside. Whenever our teasing and heckling became too pungent, Mother would pretend to scold us, ending always with 'You donkeys!'.

As soon as Maamanaar sat down, Amma quickly got up and bustled off to the kitchen. Appa scurried behind her, meek as a baby goat, but intent on seeing what she was up to. When she returned a little later down the long passage from the kitchen, bearing aloft in one hand a silver tumbler full of buttermilk flavoured with asafoetida, Appa was right behind. Unseen by both sister and brother and entirely for our delight, he made faces and minced along, mimicking her walk exactly, with his empty hand holding up an imaginary tumbler: 'It seems her brother has come on a visit! Look at her fussing over him and serving buttermilk!' he seemed to be saying.

The aroma of asafoetida in the buttermilk made us want to have some right away. We were quite certain it must be just to drink buttermilk that Maamanaar came to our house so often. The buttermilk from our cow was divine nectar, no less. And Maamanaar was the worst miser in town; we believed he was so greedy he would never give anything away free.

Maamanaar had bought that milch cow for his little sister, our *Amma*, at the *Kannavaram* cattle fair. Whenever he came over and also just before he left, he'd go up to the shed and walk around the cow, give it a pat and some words of praise. Always few and frugal. For Maamanaar was wary of the evil eye and didn't want his own too-ardent look to bring ill-luck upon it.

My youngest brother and sister doted on its little calf. 'As soon as the milk dries up he's going to take the cow back ... and the calf will go back with it!' My little siblings' fearful anticipation of this separation increased their fondness for the calf and their bitter feelings for Maamanaar. The baleful glare from their two small faces should have pricked and pinched him all over. But there he was, drinking his buttermilk with relish.

Maamanaar showed a lively interest in the deliberations about the chair and let it be known that he would like one made for himself as well. We, too, were glad of some support in our enterprise.

'Neem wood is best,' he declared. 'Keeps the body cool. No one who sits on a neem-wood chair will ever suffer from piles.'

When he mentioned the neem tree, Appa covertly flashed him an astonished glance. Appa had been talking to our farmhand only the day before yesterday about cutting down the ancient neem and laying it out to dry! Its wood had seasoned and become diamond-hard over long years of standing in the unwatered cattle-pasture.

Peddanna said, 'Making it out of a *poovarasu* log would be really good. That's a firm, fine-grained wood, without knots. It'll be fine and glossy. And strong, too.'

Our elder sister said, 'All those woods have a whitish colour. Horrible to look at! After a few days we ourselves will start hating the sight of them. So what I'm saying is, better make it out of some wood with a dark colour. Like red sugarcane ... or sesame oilcake ... But then it's your wish.' A luxury chair, fashioned out of some shiny black wood with a mirror-like gleam, with carved front legs, a back curved to support a reclining spine, rear legs stretching as though yawning languorously ... the vision flashed before our eyes and faded away.

It struck everyone that what she said was absolutely right. And so it was at once arranged for two such chairs to be made, one for us and another for Maamanaar. When both chairs were finished and delivered at our house, we didn't know which one to keep for ourselves and which to send to Maamanaar's house. If you saw one, you didn't need to look at the other. They were like Rama and Lakshmana. Finally we sent one off to Maamanaar's. And at once there was the doubt: had we sent away the better of the two?

One by one each of us tried out the chair—and didn't have the heart to rise from it. Each felt obliged to get up only because the next person had to have a chance. Peddanna sank into it with an appreciative 'Ah ... h', rubbed his hands on its smooth arms, tucked up his legs and folded them under him. Athai said, 'We have to stitch a cover for it at once, or it'll get dirty.'

My youngest brother and sister fought over it all the time. 'You've been sitting on it for so long already! Get up, da! It's my turn now!' she'd shout at him.

'Ayyo, I've just sat down! Look at her, Amma!' he'd say, crinkling up his face as though he were going to cry.

Like fire the news spread all over the village that a chair had come into our house. Grown-ups and children came crowding in to have a look at it. Some ran their hands over it. One elderly person picked it up.

'Quite heavy! He's made it sturdy,' he said in praise of the carpenter.

Some days passed. One night, at around two, someone banged on our door. Peddanna, who was sleeping on the inside verandah, opened the door. An important person in the village had just died, they said. Our chair was needed, they said, and took it away with them.

Since the deceased was someone of consequence to us, we went as a family to attend the funeral. But when we went to the house of mourning, what a sight met our eyes! It was on our chair that they had propped up that eminent personage for his last journey!

So far, whoever died in our village had always been made to sit on the floor. A grinding stone would be laid on the ground and propped up to keep it from rolling away, and braced upon it would be a gunny sack stuffed with millet straw. On this slanting bolster the corpse would be placed, as though it were reclining.

Where our village people had now picked up this new-fangled notion of seating corpses in chairs, we had no idea. People had moved from floor-tickets in cinema halls to chair-tickets ... whatever the cause, that was the beginning of our chair's tribulations.

When the 'festivities' in that household were over, they dropped our chair off in our frontyard. Just looking at it gave the children a fright. We had the servant take it to the well at the back, scrub it down with a handful of straw and wash it with fifteen large buckets of water. For several days no one had the courage to sit on it. We just didn't know how to make it usable once more.

Fortunately, one day a visitor came to our house. The chair was ordered in for him, but he said, 'Don't bother. I'll just sit down here!' and went towards the cloth mat.

Alarmed that he would seat himself there and neglect the chair, the entire family rushed up to him to persuade him to sit on it. The moment he did so, my little brother and sister fled to the backyard. Then they kept peeping in from time to time to see if anything had happened to him.

It was not until the next day, when a local elder dropped by and happened to sit on it, that we were reassured of its safety. 'Already he's practising how it'll feel!' Peddanna said secretly into my ear.

This was the way we had the chair 'seasoned' once again: the old people in the house sat on it first. The little ones were still afraid. 'Please sit down a bit first!' my big sister would beg my younger brother. 'Why can't you sit down first?' he'd snap back.

It wasn't until Suganthi, the girl who lived in the next street came over and seated her one-year-old baby brother on the chair that the children began sitting on it without fear.

Again, one night somebody died and they carried the chair away. This began to happen more and more often. Sadly we let them take it away each time. The mourners who came asking for the chair understood our sorrow quite differently: They would assume we too were mourning the death of their kinsman.

It was irritating too, to have our sleep disturbed. 'Don't know why these wretched people have to go and die at such unearthly hours!' said my elder sister one night.

'A fine chair we've made—for every corpse in the village to sit on! Tchai!' said Peddanna wearily.

'The chair was ordered at an unlucky hour,' Athai declared.

Peddanna finally came up with an idea. He and I decided to keep it to ourselves.

One day Amma sent me on some errand to Maamanaar's house. When I entered, there he was, seated in splendour on his chair and chewing betel. Watching him prepare and chew a wad of betel was an interesting pastime in itself. Carefully, with the utmost delicacy so as not to injure it in the slightest, he would open his brass betel box. A span wide, an elbow long, and four fingers high, this prized casket was cleaned and burnished every day till it shone like gold. Taking out the betel leaves one by one as if he were taking things out of a pooja box, he would lay them out with the devotion due to objects of worship. Though he would thoroughly wipe each leaf, he never pinched off the stalks (such was his parsimony!). Whenever he found a coarse-textured leaf, he would strip off the veins running along its spine. Which made us always think of the whimsical riddle:

Grab Muthappan, strip off his spine
Smear him with 'butter', fresh and new
Bite into him and chew-chew, chew-chew!

Butter, of course, meant white lime paste.

Next, he would sniff the broken areca nut. Smelling it is supposed to ward off the strange, trance-like sensation that you can get chewing on a mouthful of areca nut. Then he would blow on it. That was for getting rid of any invisible areca-nut worms. This sniffing and blowing procedure was repeated several times, his hand transporting the areca nut from nose to mouth, nose to mouth, more and more rapidly, until oomm-oosh, oomm-oosh, oomm-oosh, oomm-oosh, dabak! into his mouth the areca nut would go, having been noisily purified.

To find out how clean a person is, all one needs is to take a look at the box in which he keeps lime paste for his betel. Maamanaar was a nonpareil in this respect. Not for him the wasteful and messy habit of wiping the excess on his fingers upon the nearest wall. You could press his lime box to your eyes in reverence, it was so clean. His Eveready flashlight, purchased a full fifteen years ago, looked as though it had just been brought home from the shop; he had looked after it so well. But the one acquired by our family at exactly the same time had sprung a leak. It was all dented and of a pitiable yellow colour, like a person who has been ailing for a very long time and is about to die.

That chair could be used by no one but himself in that house. First thing in the morning he would dust it himself. If it had to be moved, he would do it himself, very gently setting it down soundlessly, as though it were an earthern pot full of water.

As soon as he set eyes on me, Maamanaar said hospitably, 'Do come in *Maapillai*! Would you perhaps like to chew some betel?' Answering his own question, he added, 'When schoolboys start chewing betel, chickens will grow horns and start butting us!'

I gave him Amma's message and went home.

That night, at an untimely hour, there was a knock at the door. Everyone in the house was fast asleep. I woke up Peddanna. Some people from a house of bereavement stood waiting outside. Peddanna led them out into the street. I went along too. When they had finished telling us what they had come for, he coolly replied: 'Oh, the chair ...? It is in our Maamanaar's house. Go and ask him. He'll give it.' Having sent them away we came back inside and laughed noiselessly.

Fuzzy with sleep, Appa turned in bed and asked, 'Who came?'

'Oh, someone wants to borrow our ... bullocks for threshing, what else?' Peddanna said. Pulling the sheet over himself, Appa rolled over to the other side.

The deluge had shifted course—now it was Maamanaar's turn to be swamped!

Several days later when I went to Maamanaar's house, he was sitting on the floor and chewing betel. He greeted me with his habitual smile and chatter.

'Why, you're on the floor! Where's the chair?' I looked around.

As he spread lime on the back of a betel leaf, he gave me a probing look and smiled. Then he said, serenely, 'I told them to keep the chair. To use it for such occasions. A chair's needed for *that* too, isn't it?'

I just didn't know what to say. Returning home I rushed in, intending to tell Peddanna this piece of news. But somehow my feet gradually slowed down by themselves.

Translated by Vasantha Surya

GLOSSARY

maamanaar   The boys already address their maternal uncle or Mama as Maamanaar or father-in-law because cross-cousin marriages (between children of a brother and a sister) were taken for granted.

maapillai   son-in-law.

pillaiyaar   popular Tamil synonym for the god Ganesha.

poovarasu   a type of tree.

QUESTIONS FOR DISCUSSION

Reading the Story

1. Did you find this story funny? Comment on how the author successfully employs humour to bring alive all the elements of short fiction—the setting, the characters, the era, etc.

2. Notice how the author introduces serious undertones to the story with such a light touch. How does he achieve this effect?

3. Characterization is so important to this story. Is Maamanaar firmly etched in your mind? Or is he merely an object of fun? How does

the author weave in the unexpected depths to his character? Did you ever think that the story would end this way?

4. There are vivid descriptions in this story, especially of the characters, who seem to pulsate with life. Study any one character carefully and discuss the role of description in the characterization.

5. Would you agree that the chair too is a character in this story? Elaborate on its importance and place in the story.

6. How does the author bring alive the times?

7. A story like this can never be dated, and it is not difficult to identify with it. How does the author make the story work for a contemporary reader?

8. How did the title prepare you for what followed in the story?

Translation Issues

9. Did you ever feel that it was a translation that you were reading? If so, what was it in the story that drew your attention to this fact?

10. Notice the use of kinship terms (maamanaar, athai, peddanna), Tamil expressions, etc. How do they enrich the story?

Activities

11. Take a funny, descriptive story in any one of the Indian languages. Translate a page that interests you (a team effort might be more interesting). Discuss the meanings of words closely. Did you have different views on translation?

12. Try a little exercise in description (it could be anything: a situation, an object, a place, or a character). But choose an era or a setting different from your own. Make sure that you have researched to get the details right.

13. Write this story from the point of view of the chair.

TELUGU

ABBURI CHAYA DEVI (b. 1933)

Hailed as one the earliest feminist writers in Telugu, Abburi Chaya Devi's work has been widely anthologized. Her family was extremely orthodox and she took to writing as a means of self-expression. She edited *Vanitha*, a monthly Telugu journal. In 2005, Abburi Chaya Devi won the Sahitya Akademi award. She served as Librarian at the Jawaharlal Nehru University.

స్పర్శ

చెప్పులు వీధి గుమ్మంలోనే విడిచి వెళ్ళానేమో, నేను వచ్చినట్లు ఏ విధమైన శబ్దమూ కాలేదు. మంచం దగ్గరగా వెళ్ళి, "పడుకున్నారా?" అన్నాను.

"ఎవరూ?" అంటూ ఇటువైపుకి ఒత్తిగిల్లారు.

"నేనే," అన్నాను.

"రా, ఇలా కూర్చో" అన్నారు పడుకునే. నేను అక్కడున్న ఒక స్టీలు కుర్చీ కొంచెం పక్కకి లాగి కూర్చోబోతుంటే ఆ చప్పుడు విని, "అంత దూరంలో ఎందుకు? ఇలా వచ్చి కూర్చోవమ్మా," అంటూ, మంచం మీద తను లేచి కూర్చుని, నాకు తన పక్కన చోటు చూపించారు చేత్తో మంచం మీద తట్టుతూ.

నేను వెళ్ళి మంచం పట్టె మీద కూర్చున్నాను.

నాన్నగారు చేత్తో తడుముతూ నా వీపు మీద చెయ్యి వేసి, తన పక్కన మంచం మీద తడిమి, "సరిగ్గా కూర్చోమ్మా," అన్నారు.

నేను కొంచెం వెనక్కి జరిగి సర్దుకున్నాను.

ఆయన చేత్తో తడుముతూ, నా చెయ్యి అందుకుని తన చేతుల మధ్య పెట్టుకుని, "నువ్వొస్తావని రోజూ ఎదురుచూస్తున్నాను. అంతా కులాసాగా ఉన్నారా?" అన్నారు.

"ఊ," అన్నాను సన్నగా.

ఆయన ఇంకేమీ మాట్లాడకుండా నా చెయ్యి నిమురుతూ నిశ్శబ్దంగా ఉండిపోయారు.

ఇది వరకోసారి – అంటే, నేను యుక్తవయస్సులో ఉన్నప్పుడు – నాన్నగారు, నేను ఒకే రిక్షాలో వెళ్ళవలసి వచ్చింది ఎక్కడికో. రిక్షా విశాలంగా ఉన్నా, నేను ఒకవైపుకి బాగా ఒదిగి కూర్చున్నాను.

"సరిగ్గా కూర్చోమ్మా పడిపోతావు." అన్నారు నాన్నగారు.

The Touch*

When I arrived, I found father lying out on the string cot, facing the wall. I had left my slippers outside on the threshold. So my footsteps did not give away my presence. I went right up to the cot and asked, 'Are you asleep?'

'Who is it?' he asked as he turned on his side.

'It's I,' I replied.

'Come, sit here,' he said, continuing to lie stretched out. When he heard me pulling the steel chair and preparing to sit down, he asked, 'Why do you want to sit so far away? Come and sit close to me.' He sat up to make space for me, patting the place on the cot next to him.

I sat on the edge of the cot.

Groping, father patted me on my back, then he felt the place next to him on the cot and said, 'Sit comfortably, amma.'

I shifted a little, making myself comfortable.

He groped the air in front of him, gripped my hand, held it in both his, and said, 'I have been looking forward to your visit. Is everyone all right?'

'Yes,' I said softly.

He didn't say anything else and silently stroked my hand.

Once, as a teenager, we had to go somewhere in a rickshaw. Though the rickshaw was spacious, I sat huddled at the far end.

'Sit properly amma, you'll fall off,' father had said.

I had hesitated and moved just an inch closer to him.

From the time I learnt my first letters of the alphabet, father had kept me at a distance—in the name of discipline, and because of *madi*, his orthodox way of life. I never had the courage to touch him. I had always felt that he was in a state of ritual purity. I was used to slipping into my cocoon. So how could I ever think of sitting close to him in the rickshaw, our bodies touching?

---

*Sparsha

When children return from school, if you embrace them lovingly and casually question them they open up and chirp like happy birds. Instead, if they are greeted harshly at the threshold with 'How much did you score in Maths?' or 'Have you brought your report card?' they die of fright. I died many such deaths over some twenty years. I still haven't got over the diffidence they created.

Father is over eighty now. Past the age of recovering his sight even if his eyes were to be operated upon. Though he is otherwise healthy, his poor eyesight has made him weak. He has spent the last two years in bed.

My husband and I had come to town on hearing that my mother-in-law was not well, to spend time with her. I managed to visit my parents once in a while as they live in the same town. On such visits I spend about half an hour chatting with father.

To sit close to father is to revive a faint memory of childhood. When he took my hand into his and stroked it with love, the longing I had felt as a child for such a touch flooded my inner being and tears welled in my eyes. I choked; I couldn't speak. Would he understand that I had once longed for his loving touch?

Perhaps all the love and affection that had flowed between us in letters evaporated at his sharp intense look whenever we came face to face. Even in early childhood I used to avoid him to escape his piercing glances that had hurt like scorching sunrays. Now, though I knew that they had been extinguished, why was I still unable to feel free with him?

The first time I visited him in his illness, I noticed bugs on the cot. I had picked up a couple of them and silently crushed them underfoot.

Later my husband noticed a bug on our bed and had been upset. I told him that it had probably crept into my clothes when I had sat on my father's bed.

As I was leaving that day to visit my father, my husband cautioned me not to sit on my father's bed but to pull up a chair and sit a little away.

As I pulled my chair away, father asked me to sit closer to him! How could I not? He was not happy until I was almost leaning against him and had his hands in mine.

Father had longed for sons all his life but was now left with only his daughters. At the end of his life he had lost his grown son and the perpetuator of his name. Perhaps that is what destiny means! When my brother died, I had hesitated to face my father—some unknown feeling of guilt had held me back. I had felt like taking him in my arms and reassuring him, saying, 'Don't worry, I am here.' But I hesitated even to touch him. That's how I had been raised.

After I chatted with him for a while, he asked me to clip his nails. Asking mother to do it would be as useless as the mortar weeping on the shoulder of the drum. His brother was not alive to do it nor were his children around.

Not that he couldn't ask my sister-in-law, but perhaps he wanted me to do something for him. I was elated and did the job carefully.

Perhaps father was feeling depressed. He stroked my hand and said, 'It would be so nice if you moved into this town. I could stay with you.' I looked at him helplessly. A look he couldn't see. I couldn't reassure him with words either.

Father didn't speak again, and was silent as he stroked my hand. At that moment my education, my job, and everything else appeared vain and superficial. I sat for a while before leaving.

As I returned in the rickshaw, father's tender touch haunted me. Tears welled in my eyes and blurred my view of the road.

Translated by Jayashree Mohanraj

GLOSSARY

madi   ritual purity practised by orthodox Hindus.

QUESTIONS FOR DISCUSSION

Reading the Story

1. What struck you most about this story?
2. Would you agree that this is a strongly reflective story about old age and very true to life?
3. Who, according to you, is the protagonist of the story?
4. Even though this story is in the first person, it also gives us a sympathetic account of the father's predicament. Comment.
5. What was the narrator's childhood like?
6. Do you think the father was shaped by his own upbringing? Give evidences from the text to show that he may have preferred to be a little more demonstrative about his affection?

7. The concept of madi or ritual purity is central to the father's character. In what way does it impinge on his life?
8. In such a short story, Abburi Chaya Devi brings out so many facets of life. What light does she throw on parenting, patriarchy, orthodoxy, and the helplessness of old age?

Translation Issues

9. The expression, 'the mortar weeping on the shoulder of the drum' is evocative. The mortar and the drum are both pounded; therefore neither can seek sympathy from the other; both are victims. Would it have been bland had an English equivalent been used? Are there similar expressions in your own mother tongue?
10. Terms such as madi are often difficult to capture in English. Are you aware of any other such concepts that defy easy translation?

Activities

11. Have you met like people like the narrator's father? Give a brief descriptive account.
12. Pick any other story (translated into English from any Indian language) about old age. How has that author treated it?
13. Talk to an elderly person who doesn't know English about old age. Make a note of their views and put them into a crisp paragraph in English.

RAAVI SASTRY (1922–93)

Rachakonda Viswanathasastry, popularly known as Raavi Sastry, is best known for his *Aaru Saaraa Kathalu,* a short story collection, and his novel *Apajeevi.* Winner of the Sahitya Akademi Prize, Raavi Sastry's literary career spanned fifty odd years. Writer, lawyer, and socio-political activist, his writings reflect his deep concern for the downtrodden. His play *Nijam* was instrumental in bringing about a change in the laws relating to rape. He was associated both with *Arasam* (Progressive Writers Association) as well as with *Airasam* (Revolutionary Writers Association). He was one of the early writers who used dialect to good effect.

వర్షం

వర్షం దబాయించి జబర్దస్తీ చేస్తోంది. సాయంకాలం అవుతోంది. మబ్బుల వల్ల మామూలు కంటే, చీకటి ఎక్కువగా వుంది. రోడ్డు పక్క కమ్మలపాక – టీ దుకాణంలో చీకటి చిక్కగా ఉంది. అడివిపాలెం నుంచి వచ్చి తన దుకాణంలో చిక్కుకుపోయిన సిటీబాబుని ఉద్దేశించి,

"మూడ్రోజులక్కాని ఒగ్గదీ ఒరనం," అన్నాడు దుకాణం తాత. ఒగ్గితే సెవి కదపాయిస్తాన్నాడు.

బల్ల మీద దిగులుబడి కూర్చుండిపోయేడు, సిటీబాబు అనబడే పురుషోత్తం.

"టేసన్కి కదు బాబు ఎళ్ళాలన్నావు?"

ఆకాశం మెరుపుతో చీల్చుకొంది.

"అవును."

"అబ్బో! ఎక్కడ, రౌండు కోసులుందే!"

పిడుగు పడ్డట్టుగా ఉరిమింది.

"ఏమిటీ?"

"రౌండు కోసులందయ్యా బాబూ! బొగ్గుల కోసం కుట్టోళ్ళి అక్కడికే తగిల్నాను సదుపుకోనేదు గాని నాకెరికే, రెండు కోసులుంది," అది రెండువేల మైళ్ళ దూరం అన్నట్టుగా చెప్పాడు దుకాణం తాత.

"బస్సు దొరకదా?" అని హీన స్వరంతో అడిగాడు పురుషోత్తం.

"ఈ వర్షంలో బస్సు రాగల్దా? ఎల్రేటి నీకు – ఉత్తప్పుడే రాదు. మా కుర్రాడు నడిసే ఎళ్ళాడు." పురుషోత్తానికి కొంచెం గాభరా వేసింది. అత్యవసరమైన పని మీద అతను కలకత్తా వెళ్ళవలసి ఉంది. మూడురోజుల లోపల అక్కడికి వెళ్ళాలి అంటే మరో రెండు గంటల్లో అతను స్టేషన్ చేరుకోవాలి. బస్సు రాదట. బళ్ళు కనిపించవు. వర్షం చూస్తే పెను ప్రళయంలా ఉంది.

"నేను కలకత్తా వెళ్ళాలే."

"ఏ వూరూ?"

"కలకత్తా"

"అబ్బో! సాన దూరవే అక్కడి కెళ్ళాలా నువ్వ?"

"అవును"

"ఎళ్ళలేవు"

Rain*

Like a big bully, the rain kept up its coercion. It was towards evening. Because of the overcast sky, it was darker than usual. In the thatched tea shack by the roadside, the gloom was more irksome. Addressing the city gent who had arrived from Adivipalem and been trapped in his tea shack, the old man observed:

'This rain won't stop for three days.' He added that he would bet his ear on it.

Feeling uneasy, Purushottam, otherwise called 'city gent', sank onto the bench.

'You said you are going to the railway station?'

The sky was split by lightning.

'Yes.'

'Too much! It is at least two *cos*!'

It thundered as though lightning had struck.

'What?'

'I am saying it is at least two cos. I rushed my boy there for fetching coal. I am not lettered. But I am sure it is two cos,' said the old one, making it sound like two thousand miles.

'Can't I get a bus?' asked Purushottam in a feeble voice.

'You think the bus can come in this kind of rain? Are you out of your mind? Even in normal times, it does not come. My boy went on foot.'

Purushottam grew rather worried. He had to go to Calcutta on urgent business. If he had to reach Calcutta within three days, he must reach the railway station within the next two hours. The bus had been ruled out—he could not even see a cart anywhere. The rain, on the other hand, was coming down like the deluge.

'I must go to Calcutta, but how?'

'Which place?'

---

*Varsham

'Calcutta.'

'Oho, that is very far off. You have to go there?'

'Yes.'

'You cannot.'

The old man had expressed himself with great certainty. Purushottam sat dejected. Lightning kept flashing like naked swords. Thunder roared and kept roaring as though it was determined to split the hills. In a wild frenzy, the gale blew. The rain came down with a vengeance. The shack had been taken over by the gloom, but the new trousers, the new shirt, and the new shoes stood out. All these Purushottam was wearing. Had anyone wanted to take a better look at him, he would have had to light a lamp. Was he handsome? Not many would agree that he was. But it must be conceded that he had a slender, attractive waist. He might have been lion-waisted, but not lion-hearted. When he was fifteen, many wondered if he was not twenty. If the opinion of the tea-shack man were sought, he might have said, 'Closer to forty.' That Purushottam had been born only twenty-five years ago was not known to any other than those who knew about his birth. Like a calf that failed to grow, he remained stunted.

His journey, before he got stuck in that tea-shack, had started the day before. He had actually started for Calcutta. But from somewhere arrived, like a dust devil, his maternal uncle. This uncle specialized in giving unsolicited advice to people; wouldn't find it hard to set people to tasks. Now he descended on the young man and confronted him. 'Do you know that you have to get married?' he hustled him, 'Hurry, hurry, move, go. Good girl, nubile girl, wealthy girl. The daughter of the munsif in Adivipalem is waiting. After bride-viewing, you can proceed to Calcutta without any problem. Go, go, go, and see her.' He fairly chased his nephew into this. After that, the young man, bag in hand, landed in a relative's house in Adivipalem and putting on his new clothes, materialized in the evening before the would-be bride. She looked at him once and that one look presented a formidable poser to him.

The 'muneeseeb' lived in an old-fashioned tiled house. On a mat on the rear verandah, they presented the girl. There she sat comfortably, at ease, cross-legged. Not far off, next to the sacred *tulasi* plant, a white sari was drying on a clothesline. In the yard, wet brass utensils, freshly scrubbed and washed, glinted. He could even see a mango tree behind the house, dark and green. Next to it, right next to it, stood a coconut palm, tall and straight and majestic, as though ready to make the ultimate sacrifice to protect the mango tree. In two minds, whether to set or not, the sun in the sky hovered near the rear door. All of a sudden, he felt that someone had thrown open all the doors and windows and spilled tones of vermilion all over the sky. At that, the tender shoot on the mango tree and the fronds on the coconut palm rejoiced quietly. The white sari on the clothesline caught the diffused light and splashed the whole place with the red. The brass utensils, already shiny, now assimilated a little of copper and shimmered like gold. In its brickwork pot, the tulasi plant stood poised like a classical danseuse.

In the lamplight, the would-be bride looked the very image of the goddess Devi. Her head slightly lowered, eyelids lifted a little, she took a good deliberate look at Purushottam. Those eyes looked like two ponds filled to the brim with fresh and pure water. Though bred and brought up in a remote village, those eyes had grown to see clearly the shining stars, the bright moon, and the burning sun as well. And they could see far.

The mother was throwing all sorts of questions at her daughter and getting her to talk. The girl spoke softly, but those words sounded lofty and solemn, like words spoken in a cave. At the conclusion of the interview, as Purushottam rose to leave, she looked at him again with that same poise from where she was sitting on the mat, raising her eyelids slightly, heavily. On the conclusion of that assessment, she went in. Her look started an agitation in his breast, though he could not figure out why.

Next day, after the midday meal at the relative's house, he climbed into a double-bullock cart and headed towards the road junction. It was one in the afternoon. Tinkling their neckbells, the bullocks surged forward. As the cart went by the munsif's house which was right on the way, for some reason the would-be bride came out into the street, saw the cart, and instead of turning promptly back, kept standing there. Leaning one arm on the doorframe, she stood there firmly and looked steadily at him. The cart moved on. She was left behind; but that look of hers kept chasing him; putting it in other words, that look burrowed deep pits in him. Sometime earlier, Purushottam had fallen ill and was hospitalized. He was terribly weak and emaciated. From behind the doctors examining him, a nurse stepped out and said, 'Come with me,' and took him to a weighing machine. As they moved, he noticed she was looking at him. She was of tender age. The sick environment around her had not yet made her insensitive. Her eyes were quite small. The meaning of her look he did not understand until he had weighed himself on the machine. Then he realized, 'That's it, she had been trying to estimate my weight!' When he stepped down from the machine, she looked at him with pity and gave him a cautioning smile and said, 'Nothing to worry. Rest assured. You will be normal in no time.' He hadn't known how to thank her and his eyes had brimmed. As he now sat on the cart, somehow Purushottam remembered that sensitive nurse. Viewing the dark hills in the distance, the coconut groves this side, next to them the green fields, overhead the silver spread of the clouds, he was lost in his thoughts. Am I the correct weight? He asked himself. But he could not make sense of it. Like wet firewood, his mind was taking time to ignite. The cart moved steadily on. When the cartman pulled the bullocks to a stop—'Ohoy, hoy, hoy'—he started up and got down. At the same moment, somewhere the sky roared, reverberated. In the orchards, the breeze fluttered; it whirled. Purushottam looked at the sky. The wind had swept the sky clean of the white clouds. From the other side, dark clouds streamed out, like lava, like a tidal wave, on a rampage.

Where the *kutcha* road joined the trunk road, standing like a government officer by the roadside a tamarind stoutly defied the skies. Under the tamarind tree stood the tea-shack shaking like an old woman in the cold. In no time, the clouds had covered the heavens. Like moisture on a child's slate exposed to the sun, the sunlight disappeared even as he watched, while the shadows of the clouds raced across the fields.

The cartman threw obscenities at the wind and dust, turned the cart around and jumped onto his seat. Defying the dust and breeze, the bullocks raced home. As Purushottam rushed into the tea-shack opposite, rain descended in a spatter and bustle. The breeze grew into a gale and the rain came down like a flood surging into low-lying land, drenched the hut in no time, and moved forward with a roar.

Purushottam had sat on the tea-shack bench for over an hour. The tumblers lay idly on the table. What looked like a kettle had gone to sleep on the fireplace; the fire below was dying out rapidly. The whole tea-shack looked quite indolent. Appearing as though it was not his job to prepare tea, the old man sat on his three-legged stool like an aged cat, sucked twice at his already dead cheroot, put it down on the table without relighting it, and said, 'Where are you from?' And that was his first question. He followed that up with the whole series, dropping them steadily—like rainwater descending from thatch eaves, he dropped them on Purushottam. Dreading the consequences if he failed to respond, he answered each and every question.

At the end of it all, the old man told him with utmost certainty that he would not be able to reach his destination and then smiled to himself with satisfaction.

The rain grew; the gale blew. Lightning tore open the heavens; thunder exploded. The hills stood defying the onslaught. The trees were in revolt. The fire in the shack's hearth was not getting enough air; on top of it, the roof leaked, water dripped from the kettle into the embers below and evaporated.

Suppressing his smile in his days-old beard, the old man said, 'He went for coal, the boy. Has not returned yet, where he is stuck, who knows?'

'Do you mean to say the bus won't turn up today?'

'If you think of it, even the train won't move today in this rain. Not to speak of the useless bus,' the old man said, and he appeared quite pleased that the whole world had been paralysed by the deluge.

The rain and wind sounded like so many snakes crawling down the thatched roof of the shack. Not even two hours left for the arrival of the train at the nearest station.

'If only you had started earlier, you could have made it on foot. Now you cannot reach it. The whole world is just one flood now.'

The old fellow appeared pleased too that he would not be able to make it even on foot.

In agony, Purushottam continued to sit. The old man was vexed that the boy who had gone to fetch coal had not returned yet. The hut was now soaked. It grew colder, the cold breeze grew wilder.

The rain poured down.

'Why should it not rain? Rain has to come at its proper time.'

Now less than two hours from the arrival of the train, he was still the same two cos away from the station as earlier. The bus must have been stranded somewhere. The sky was breaking up. Purushottam stood up.

'No human creature can step outside.'

Purushottam moved about restlessly, chafing at being forced to do nothing.

'Do you have matches?'

'No.'

'I thought as much. The only way you can get a fire now is to make it out of water. And this fellow has not returned. He is only a boy. The fellow is a daredevil though. He can defy the rain, why only the rain, he can bear down a whole herd of elephants on the way.'

Purushottam's thoughts were far away from the boy, his departure for coal, any confrontation with elephants. To him the tea-shack appeared like a narrow prison cell; the steadily descending rain like so many bars. He was quite distraught, cursing his situation.

'Go, go!' Someone had said and he had obeyed. He should have first gone to Calcutta, settled his matters there, and then come to view the girl. It had been that way, ever and always. That chit of a girl appeared to have assessed him correctly. Tcha, he had always been like this! 'You must come to Calcutta,' they said; 'I shall,' he said. 'Go to Adivipalem,' said the uncle. 'Going,' he said. He had been like this since his childhood. 'If you don't study well, you will come to no good, so study well,' they said; he agreed. 'Watch your conduct, otherwise you will come to no good,' they said; he swore by the gods to behave himself. A friend mocked him: 'people who don't know how to enjoy life behave properly,' he said; Purushottam concurred. This had been his style, his approach in every matter. 'If you don't know how to swim, don't get into water, be careful.' 'Of course, I won't!' 'Don't walk in the dark without a lamp in your hand, be cautious!' 'Of course, I won't!' 'Walk on the highways and not in lanes and bylanes, take care!' 'Of course.' 'Let others drop dead, but you don't go to their help!' 'Of course, I won't.' 'Inequity and injustice: why bother about it , mind your own business, otherwise you will land yourself in serious trouble, so take care.' 'True, why bother about these things; why court unnecessary trouble? I shall mind my business!' 'Typhoid, pneumonia, or some other disease you will catch, so don't go out in the rain, be careful!' 'Of course, I won't go out in the rain, I shall remain here.'

Purushottam woke up with a start. Then how was he going to reach Calcutta? Not more than an hour and a half was left. Undecided on a course of action, he was about to drop down on the bench again when the old man shouted with joy, 'Here he comes! That's it, just like a hound! Come fast, run quickly!'

Purushottam bent low and peeped out.

He could see the road straight and open before him. On either side stood trees, soaring like soldiers, now agitated. The entire length of the road was one sheet of water, looked like a canal. All alone on this road, like an unquenchable ember, like a smooth-sailing boat on the water, as though tearing apart the trees to make his way down, the bag flung on his shoulder, came surging, a boy.

Having cheered on the boy, the old man turned and puffing his cheeks out blew with all his might into the fire. 'I thought the fire had died out. No, there is still a spark left,' he said and began to blow more furiously than ever.

The boy came up fast, cutting through the rain and with one bound burst into the shack. 'I made it Grandfather!' he shouted as he entered, easily slipped the bag from his shoulder and dropped it quickly on the floor. The boy was not above twelve years of age—exactly like a hound. In no time he squeezed the water out of his hair, squeezed his clothes dry, and kept hopping around the shack with unbounded energy. 'If you had died somewhere in the rain, what would you have done, Grandson?' the old man asked opening the coal bag. As he opened the bag, the hard coal glinted and shone. 'Rain! Don't you know me, grandfather. This Pothuraju can knock off any rain,' said the boy as though he was the lord of all the three worlds, and moved off jauntily to blow into the fire. Purushottam stood as though rooted in that shack. The sky flashed. The would-be bride who had haunted him all along now stood right before him. That look she had given him, that smile, that half-smile that tender nurse had given him; the mango tree just putting out new shoots, the soaring coconut palm; cold wind, torrential rain; fire out of water, the flame in man—he now understood everything. It all made sense, clear and vivid, like a story on the screen. He now understood everything. In contemplation of it all, he stood still.

Streams of rain appeared as though they were hanging still and immobile. The sky was, rather than clearing, becoming more overcast. The cold wind raged as though driving an unstoppable all-crushing chariot. The flashes of light were followed by lightning, destroying anything and everything around. The more the clouds gathered, the darker it became in the tea-shack.

The boy fanning the fire now looked inflamed like red hot iron.

The old man, now bustling around the shack, suddenly seemed to remember something, stopped short, narrowed his eyes, looked around, and addressed his grandson, 'Look here, he was here until a moment ago. Where has the city gent disappeared?' expressing his surprise, as though he half believed that the young fellow had been snatched away by the local deity, Ennemma.

'There!' said Pothuraju.

'Where?'

'Look, look over there,' said Pothuraju, pointing to the road.

'What!' exclaimed the old man in disbelief, bending low and peering out. 'I thought he had settled down here like a good-for-nothing. I thought he wouldn't leave the shack until the rain stopped. Aha, he did it!'

In the semi-darkness of the road ahead, straight and firm, braving the cold wind fully and squarely, unmindful of the downpour, penetrating the curtain around him, moved on Purushottam. Gazing at the sight, looking at him, the old man nodded his head and said, '*Sabaas!*'

Translated by Ranga Rao

GLOSSARY

kutcha	rough
munsif/muneseeb	judge
sabaas	well-done
tulasi	basil

QUESTIONS FOR DISCUSSION

Reading the Story

1. The very first sentence of the story is evocative of what is to follow. How does Raavi Sastry construct a rainy day for us?

2. There is a freshness in Sastry's imagery. Pick out sentences from the story that reflect the author's mastery over language.

3. Dialogue is kept to a minimum in the story. Notice the power of description. Do you agree that it is this element that carries the story forward?

4. Rain plays an important part in the story. How does it connect with Purushottam's destiny?

5. It seems as if the description of Purushottam at the beginning of the story matches his character. Comment.

6. The character of Purushottam is brilliantly etched. How does the author achieve this?

7. Would you agree that Purushottam is the average man on the street? Did you identify with him?

8. Despite growing up in a remote hamlet, the 'girl' has a certain poise and confidence that Purushottam lacks. What did you think of the 'bride-viewing' function in which the roles of prospective bride and groom are clearly reversed?

9. What effect does the dramatic entry of the boy have on the timid Purushottam?

Translation Issues

10. Idioms and proverbs convey a sense of culture, place, and people. A good translator always tries to arrive at a workable literal translation to retain the spirit of the original. Do you agree with the translator's decisions?

11. This story would have worked just as effectively in any Indian language. Most of our Indian languages share similar idioms and proverbs. Identify them in this story. Do you have equivalents in your language? Translate them into English.

Activities

12. At the end of the story, Purushottam makes a sudden decision to take charge of his life, much to the approval of the old man. Has any one situation transformed your life? Write about it.

13. Write a descriptive paragraph about rain in your mother tongue. Translate it into English.

KODAVATIGANTI KUTUMBA RAO (1909–80)

Highly versatile, it is difficult to categorize Kutumba Rao, also known as KoKu. He was a short story writer, novelist, playwright, and a highly accomplished children's writer. His writings, charming and steeped in dialect, are underscored by a strong social purpose. Kutumba Rao worked in several places from Shimla to Bombay and Madras in such positions as clerk, teacher, factory foreman, and film writer before settling down to journalism. After a stint in some papers, a few of which he founded himself, he became editor of *Chandamama*, a popular children's magazine. Kutumba Rao is unparalleled in his understanding of the sociological aspects of Andhra culture. His novel *Tara* won the Andhra Pradesh Sahitya Akademi award.

తాతయ్య

మనుషులందర్లోకి బ్రాహ్మలెక్కువ. బ్రాహ్మర్లో నియోగ్యుల కంటి వైదీకులెక్కువ. తలకాయంతా గొరిగించి వెనకాల పిలక పెట్టుకుని పొద్దున్నే మూడు వేళ్ళూ కనిపించేట్టు వీబూది పెట్టుకుని తద్దినాలు అవీ పెట్టించే బ్రాహ్మలు చాలా మంచి వాళ్ళు. వాళ్ళు అందరి ఇళ్ళకూ వచ్చి 'శ్రీకృష్ణపర్బబ్రహ్మడేనమ:' అంటారు. అప్పుడు ఇంటివాళ్ళమ్మ వచ్చి వాళ్ళ చెంబులో బియ్యం పోస్తుంది. శూద్రవాళ్ళు బిచ్చగాళ్ళు. వాళ్ళకి ముష్టి వేస్తాం. ముష్టి ఒకచేత్తో వేస్తాం. బ్రాహ్మలకి బియ్యం రెండు చేతులా, దోసిట్లో, పట్టుకొచ్చి వెయ్యాలి. వాళ్ళు ముష్టివాళ్ళు.

వాళ్ళు మీసాలుంచుకోరు. ఇస్త్రీ బట్టలు కట్టుకోరు. చొక్కాలు తొడుక్కోరు. మా తాతయ్య చొక్కా తొడుక్కునేవాడు కాదు, చలికాలంలో రాత్రిపూట తప్ప. అప్పుడు ఎర్రవాలు కుళాయి కూడా పెట్టుకునేవాడు. దాన్లోంచి మొహం మాత్రమే కనబడేది. నెత్తి, మెడ కనిపించేవి కావు. అది పెట్టుకుంటే తాతయ్య ఎవరో అల్లే ఉండేవాడు.

తాతయ్య ముష్టి ఎత్తేవాడు కాదు. తద్దినం పెట్టేటప్పుడు ఆయన కూడా బ్రాహ్మలతో పాటు మంత్రాలు చదివేవారు. తద్దినం బ్రాహ్మలు తాతయ్య కన్న ముందు తినేవాళ్ళు. అయితే తాతయ్యను వాళ్ళ అన్నం తాకనిచ్చే వాళ్ళు. తద్దినానికి గారెలు పరమాన్నమూ చేస్తారుగాని పులుసు చెయ్యరు. కంది పప్పు కూడా వండరు. పెసరపప్పు వండుతారు.

తద్దినం పెట్టించే బ్రాహ్మలంత మంచి బ్రాహ్మలు కాకపోయినా వాళ్ళు తాతయ్యను గౌరవంగా చూసేవాళ్ళు. తాతయ్యకు ఇంగ్లీష్ రాదు. అందుకని తాతయ్య నాన్నని గొప్పగా చూసేవాడు. నాన్న తాతయ్యంత మంచి బ్రాహ్మడు కాదు. నాన్నకు మీసాలుందేవి. ఇస్త్రీ బట్టలు కట్టుకునేవాడు. బిళ్ళగోచీ పెట్టుకునేవాడు కాదు. వాలు గోచీ పెట్టుకునేవాడు. తాతయ్యలా భోజనం చేసేటప్పుడు గందం అక్షింతలు పెట్టుకునేవాడు కాదు. చాచ్చుక్క పెట్టుకునేవాడు. పట్టుబట్ట కట్టుకుని భీం చేసేవాడు. పట్టుబట్ట కంటే మడిబట్టే ఎక్కువ. మడిబట్టలు ఆరేసినప్పుడు పిల్లలు ముట్టుకుంటే మైలపడతై. తడిబట్టలు మైలపడవు. కాని తడిబట్ట కన్న మడిబట్టే ఎక్కువ. దారప్పోగు తొక్కితే మడిగట్టుకున్న ముసలివాళ్ళు మైలపడతారు. పత్రికి మైలేదు.

Taatayya (My Grandpa)*

Brahmins are superior to all others. Among Brahmins, the *Vaidikis* are superior to the *Niyogis*. Those who have their heads shaved with just a tuft left at the rear, and every day, first thing in the morning, applying three fingers of sacred ash clearly seen on the foreheads, and conducting annual rites for the dead, are very pure. They come to everyone's house and say *'Sri Krishnaparabrahmaney Namaha'*. Then the mother of the family will come out and pour rice into their *chembu*. To the *sudra* fellows and beggars and others, we give alms with one hand. For the Brahmin folk, we carry the rice in both hands held together. They are not beggars.

They (Vaidikis) don't grow moustaches. They don't wear ironed clothes. Don't wear shirts. My Taatayya wouldn't wear shirts. Except during winter nights. Then he would wear a woollen cap. Only the face could be seen through it, head and neck would disappear. In it Taatayya looked like somebody else.

Taatayya would not beg for alms. On the annual-rites day he too would chant mantras with the other Brahmins. The annual-rites Brahmins would eat before Taatayya. But they allowed Taatayya to handle their food. For the annual-rites feast they cook *gaarelu* and sweetened milk rice, but they don't make *pulusu*. They will not even cook red gram. They cook green gram.

Though Taatayya was not as pure a Brahmin as the Brahmin conducting the annual rites, they respected him. Taatayya did not know English. That is why Taatayya regarded father highly. Father was not as superior a Brahmin as Taatayya. Father had a moustache. Wore pressed clothes. He wore the dhoti without the pleated end tucked up at the back. He wore it with a free-falling pleated hem. He would not apply at meals, as Taatayya did, sandalwood and sacred turmeric-

---

*Taatayya

mixed raw rice paste to his forehead. He wore a black dot on the forehead. He wore *pattu* dhoti while eating food. A *madi* cloth is superior to pattu cloth. When such purified clothes are hung out to dry, if children touch them, they are polluted. Wet clothes cannot be polluted. But the purified cloth is superior to a wet cloth. If they step on a cotton thread, the old people wearing purified clothes become polluted. Cotton wool cannot be polluted.

Sudras are far below Brahmins. They cannot be like Brahmins. They are dark. The woman who sold vegetables to us at our home was very fair. But if she spoke it became clear that she was a Sudra woman. We should not trust a black Brahmin or a fair Sudra. Taatayya of course was dark. Mother trusted him. But everyone would say that fair-skinned Sudras must never really be trusted. That woman who sold vegetables to us told mother so many tales. Mother quarrelled with her every day. Father would not quarrel with her.

Sudras eat meat. They place a chicken in the basket and pluck its feathers. While they pluck the feathers, the chicken cries for sometime. After a while it will not cry. After its feathers have been plucked, the hen cannot be recognized. Looks vile. Old Sudra women make an offering of the chicken's head to God. While making the offering, they don't chant mantras. Unlike Taatayya they don't put on purified clothes and go into a purified state. The chicken's head does not look at things like a chicken, but looks in a peculiar way at things. While the plucking is on, Brahmin children must not watch it.

Brahmin children should not drink water at houses of Sudra folk. Only if a drop of buttermilk is mixed in water can they drink it. If a drop of buttermilk is dropped in drinking water, it disappears. It will look like ordinary drinking water. The cowherd folk mix water in buttermilk. If water is mixed in buttermilk, mother will know. If Sudra folk mix water in buttermilk, Brahmins can drink it.

Niyogis are not superior Brahmins. They don't offer the *sandhya* rites. They have impure ways. If they wear that long red mark on their foreheads, they are good to look at. But that kind of forehead mark shows that they are not pure Brahmins. Children should not tell Chalapati Rao *garu* that they are not pure Brahmins. It is not proper to do so. We say it behind their backs, but when we are with them, even Niyogis are treated like pure Brahmins. We don't treat them as we do sudras. If little children drink water in the house of Niyogis it is not wrong. Little children should not ask in Niyogi homes that buttermilk be mixed with water. Elders like Taatayya would not drink water in the Niyogi home because old people don't feel thirsty.

On the occasion of any ceremony in Chalapati Rao garu's house, Taatayya will not go to the feast in their house. Mother, father, and I go. If there are annual rites or ceremonies in our house, everyone in the house of Chalapati Rao garu comes to the feast. Taatayya will eat alongside, but after they are gone he will be cross. With the coming of the railway and the trunk roads, the whole world has become pariah feed, Taatayya used to say. When Taatayya went on a journey by train, he would wear a shirt but he would not wear the cap.

After returning from the train journey, Taatayya would take off his clothes and put them apart. Father would bring in the outdoor clothes into the house. This pollution reached Taatayya of course. But what could he do? Everything is pariah feed, of course.

The Brahmins are scared of the untouchables. When the untouchables pass very close to us, we will be polluted. Some untouchables don't care even when we shout at them to warn them. They are not good untouchables. Even white people are untouchables. They don't bathe. Even though they don't bathe they are fair. Even when we wash ourselves with soap we don't look so fair. The white people are great people. Even at home they speak in English. Their ladies wear porcelain plates on their heads. Brahmins should not eat in porcelain plates. The people who eat in porcelain plates are *Saibs*.

Saibs whip cotton. When they whip cotton, it sounds nice in the beginning. Later it becomes sickening to watch. A strong man can, setting the whipping machine erect, shoot arrows from it. Saibs drive *jutka*s. They don't drive bullock carts. Saibs stitch clothes. Saibs don't do anything else. They come to the verandah-school to study. Saib musicians of the *sannai* are good to listen to. They play on the sannai at their weddings. They hang jasmine garlands against the bridegroom's face. The Saib groom goes on a horse in a procession round the town. Saib brides don't go in a procession. If they don't know how to climb a horse, Saibs don't marry.

For the celebrations of the *Peeroos,* Saibs put on the tiger mask and paint themselves and entertain people. In the festival of the Dussehra the police folk put on the costume of *betaala*s. If they look at a betaala, children are scared. The tiger show is better to watch.

The festival of *Sri Rama Navami* is also great fun. They set up thatched pandals all over the town. It is very cool under the pandals. On the day of the festival, these are full of people. Little children should not go into the crowds. The grown-ups scold them because they will lose their way back if they go into the crowds. But all that is empty talk. Children can go anywhere, they will not be lost. Because little children are short, they cannot see the God and the worship.

I like festivals the whole town joins to celebrate. In the month of *Kaartikam*, they arrange communal eating in the grove. Then people of all castes sit together and eat. Right opposite us can be seen *Vaisyas* and Sudra folk. It is good to eat like that. But it is scary. Where there is a *vusiri* tree anyone can eat without thinking of caste. There is a vusiri tree in our backyard but because of Taatayya we do not give food to Sudra folk in our house. Taatayya does not attend grove feasts either.

While celebrating *saptaaham* too all the people in the town eat together. Food is served the whole day. At night they stage *harikatha*s. Where they perform bhajans children are allowed to play on the harmonium. When children play on it, the sound comes out loud at one time and soft at another. Not just this, the hand pains. No use even if you change hands. Finally, at the end you have to use both hands. When both hands pain, you feel like crying. Even if both hands pain, we acquire merit in heaven by playing on the harmonium at a bhajan. When you cry, you are ashamed someone might see.

Great fun when the circus comes to town. Soon after the circus comes to our town, it rains. The circus tent is pitched in the fields. After the rain there is knee-deep slush in the fields. You have to wade through the slush to go the circus. They sprinkle grain chaff where people sit. When we sit on the chaff, the slush won't touch us, but the shorts get wet and it feels cold.

They sell sodas near the circus. If little children ask to drink the soda, father gets angry. Chalapathi Rao garu does not get angry. When we drink soda the mouth feels hot. It stings in the nostrils. When the marble stops the mouth of the soda bottle, you get a good feeling. It is fun to watch the circus. But there is nothing in what they do. They do things easily. Not once do they fall. But to walk on the wire holding a little umbrella is wonderfully tough. That is why that girl walks with such fear. To catch her if she falls down there will be a man. Keeps watching the girl. If the girl goes forward, he goes forward. If she moves backward, he comes back. If she runs, he runs. The girl walking on the wire looks so pretty. That man talks with the girl. That girl smiles at him. She does not smile at anyone else. Even after the circus is gone, we keep remembering her.

After the circus is gone, little children tie short strings to short sticks and make imaginary elephants dance. These string whips don't make that kind of sharp sound.

Taatayya does not like any of the festivals celebrated in the town. Even circus. Taatayya does not attend even the circus. He prefers festivals celebrated at home. Festivals at home are not as good as the festivals celebrated in the town. They make special sweet dishes but they won't allow us to eat as much as we want. Until Taatayya finishes eating, we cannot begin. On a festival day if we ask for a *gogu* chutney or *kandisunni* mother will lose her temper.

Meenakshi brings for me the sweet dishes they cook in the house of Chalapati Rao garu. Then mother looks upon Meenakshi with great affection. She even feeds Meenakshi with the sweet dishes prepared in our house. The day after the festival, mother feeds me and father with the remaining sweet dishes out of Taatayaa's sight.

If you eat too many sweet dishes, you get fever. If you get fever, you feel low. Don't feel hungry. When you have fever, and eat something without anyone watching you, the mouth feels bitter. For children running a fever, they give indigestion pills. If you swallow them you feel sick in the throat. That is a sure sign of fever.

Only children get fever. Grown-ups don't get fever. Grown-ups die. When grown-ups die, womenfolk cry. Menfolk don't cry. They look low. When they look low, they don't laugh. That alone is a sign of sadness. When Taatayya died, he didn't look dead. He looked asleep. But Taatayya snored in his sleep. Dead people don't snore. Before death they rattle a little. But when they do that kind of snoring, they are not asleep. When Taatayya snored without sleeping, mother and others poured tulasi water into his mouth. But Taatayya could not swallow the tulasi water. It got stuck between his lips. Mother wiped it away tenderly. While he was dying, mother touched Taatayya. Then father put his mouth to Taatayya's ear and chanted, 'Narayana, Narayana' and performed his *japam*.

Everyone asked father to find out what Taatayya had to say. Father does not like to ask. But when everyone asks him he asks. Father calls

Taatayya 'father'. What would you like to tell us?' father asks. When father talks thus, he seems to be someone else. Taatayya does not answer father. Goes on snoring. Even when Taatayya died his eyes were open. But like the blind beggar he did not look at anyone. I am scared of the blind beggar. When father told me about him, I felt sorry for him. He does not have a home. Does not have any fields. After hearing this I felt sorry for him. God will feel sorry for Taatayya. Because when he died he looked like the blind beggar. After his death Taatayya did not have a house or home. Taatayya was taken away somewhere. He not have fields either. Now Taatayya will not quarrel with the peasants.

Though Taatayya quarrelled with them, the peasants are not sore with him. They are Sudra folk. A peasant came and cried at Taatayya's death. When menfolk cry, it scares you. Father did not cry. When you see that he is not smiling, you know he is sad.

Taatayya has been taken by *Yama*'s men. We cannot see Yama's men. They can be seen by Taatayya. The aeroplane did not come for Taatayya. When *Naayanamma* had died, the aeroplane arrived. 'An aeroplane has come for me, I am leaving,' she herself had said. Taatayya did not say that an aeroplane had come for him. He didn't even say he was going. However pure a Brahmin Taatayya may have been, he will still go only to hell, it seems. Mother said this. However good people may be, they will do a little sin, so they will go to hell.

The world of Yama will be terrible. There Yama's men will cut dead people with saws. Strike them with maces. Burn them in fires. Boil them in hot oil. The very sight of Yama's men finishes off the dead folk. They will cut with saws those who kill hens. But cutting us is not a sin for them.

All of us, when we grow old, die like Taatayya.

Translated by Ranga Rao

GLOSSARY

betaala	fiend
bhajan	devotional Hindu songs
chembu	metal cruse
gaarelu	cookies like doughnuts made of black gram
gogu	a leafy green vegetable, Hibiscus cannabinus

harikatha	recitals of religious episodes accompanied by music and dance
japam	chanting of names (usually of God)
jutkas	small horse carriages
kandisunni	a powder made of various grams and chilli and salt
kartikam	October–November
madi	sacral
nayanamma	paternal grandmother
pandal	marquee, usually temporary
pattu	silk
pulusu	a thick soup with vegetables
saibs	Muslims
sandhya	a daily ritual practiced by orthodox Hindus (wearing the sacred thread) whose object is to bring about self-purification and divinity.
sannai	a clarinet
sapttaham	a holy week
Sri Krishnaparabrahmaney Namah	Obeisance to the Supreme Reality
sudra	low caste
Taatayya	Grand father
tulasi	sacred basil
vaisya	business caste
vusiri tree	amla tree, *Emblic myrobalan*
yama	the God of Death

QUESTIONS FOR DISCUSSION

Reading the Story

1. Point of view is very important to this story. Would it have worked from an adult perspective?
2. This is a charming, impressionistic view of a young boy's world. Which parts of the story did you find most delightful?
3. The child is clearly baffled about caste. The freshness of a child's perspective exposes the ridiculousness of prevalent customs. Pick out specific portions from the story that demonstrate this.

4. In a subtle yet convincing way, the story is an indictment of the caste system. Comment.

5. What glimpses do you get of Taatayya? Is he the epitome of middle-class life and values?

6. This is a richly textured narrative. Though the title suggests that the story is about the grandfather, it is much more than that—it is a comment on society itself. Do you agree?

7. This story is not a linear narrative. The child's world-view shuttles between past and present so effortlessly. How effective is this?

8. The strength of the story lies in its strong undercurrent of humour. It is intricately connected to the child's point of view. Comment on how the author has used humour to treat a sensitive issue like caste.

9. The descriptions in this story are vivid and evocative. Pick out any one paragraph that appeals to you and show how details seen through a child's eyes add to the richness of the story.

Translation Issues

10. In the original, the translator has explained the Telugu terms within brackets in the text itself. Would that have distracted you in any way? Are notes at the end of the story been preferable? Discuss.

11. This story revolves around castes and sub-castes, posing enormous challenges for the translator. How successfully has he coped with these challenges?

Activities

12. Pick any story from an Indian language written from a child's point of view. How does it compare with this story?

13. Notice the diction, use of tense, sentence structure, and the style of prose which capture the child's register. Write a paragraph on any experience using the first-person child's perspective.

14. Try your hand at a portrait of your own grandfather.